Where lost dogs heal lonely hearts…

Marion Lennox brings you four wonderfully warm, witty, emotional and uplifting stories with happy endings you'll never forget.

Step into Banskia Bay, a picturesque seaside town where hearts are made whole and dreams really can come true! With the help of a few mischievous little dogs, couples get together and find that they are in for journeys they had never expected….

Available now:

Abby and the Bachelor Cop
Misty and the Single Dad
Nikki and the Lone Wolf

Coming in January 2012:

Mardie and the City Surgeon

Fifteen years ago, Blake Maddock walked away from Mardie Rainey, leaving her shattered. Now he's returned and he wants to stay, but will Mardie let him back in her life?

Dear Reader,

Every night around five o'clock my dog, Mitzi, starts pacing. She starts with a mournful sigh, then trudges to the door where her lead hangs, then back to me. Over and over. Finally, I relent. Snow, sleet or baking sun, off we go to our local lake, where I let her off the lead and she can run.

And she does run—a black-and-silver mini-schnauzer, the runt of the litter, a huge dog in a little dog's body, mixing with all the other dogs who've had similar success getting their lead-holders out of their houses. We love it.

Mitzi's best mates are wolfhounds—two vast mutts who play with her as if she's an equal. She does doughnuts through their legs while I chat to their owner, Wolfhound Man, their equal in the large department—though a lot better-looking. *A lot!*

So for this story, when I needed a dog and a hero, there they were in my head—my wolfhound, Horse, and the man who loves him. Wolfhound Man has become Gabe, a sea captain and all-round hero, and of course there's Nikki, a heroine deserving of both man and dog. I'm imagining you, my reader, as my heroine, and I hope you do, too. And you don't even have to feed a wolfhound to do it.

I love the dogs in my life. I love the dogs in my books. But what I love most is when they come together with passion and laughter, and write themselves into love stories for you to enjoy with me.

Happy reading!

Marion

MARION LENNOX
Nikki and the Lone Wolf

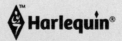

TORONTO NEW YORK LONDON
AMSTERDAM PARIS SYDNEY HAMBURG
STOCKHOLM ATHENS TOKYO MILAN MADRID
PRAGUE WARSAW BUDAPEST AUCKLAND

Recycling programs
for this product may
not exist in your area.

ISBN-13: 978-0-373-74142-7

NIKKI AND THE LONE WOLF

First North American Publication 2011

www.Harlequin.com

Printed in U.S.A.

Marion Lennox is a country girl, born on an Australian dairy farm. She moved on—mostly because the cows just weren't interested in her stories! Married to a "very special doctor", Marion writes for the Harlequin Medical™ Romance and Harlequin Romance lines (she used a different name for each category for a while—so if you're looking for her past Harlequin Romance titles, search for author Trisha David, as well). She's now had more than seventy-five romance novels accepted for publication.

In her non-writing life, Marion cares for kids, cats, dogs, chooks and goldfish. She travels, she fights her rampant garden (she's losing) and her house dust (she's lost).

Having spun in circles for the first part of her life, she's now stepped back from her "other" career, which was teaching statistics at her local university. Finally she's reprioritized her life, figured out what's important and discovered the joys of deep baths, romance and chocolate.

Preferably all at the same time!

Books by Marion Lennox

MISTY AND THE SINGLE DAD*
ABBY AND THE BACHELOR COP*

*Banksia Bay

Other titles by this author available in ebook

To Gail and to Charles, for Bob,
a gentle giant with a heart as big as he was.

CHAPTER ONE

A WOLF was at her door.

Okay, maybe it wasn't quite at her door, Nikki conceded, as she came back to earth. Or back to the sofa. The howl was close, though. Her hair felt as if it was spiking straight up, and for good reason.

It was the most appalling, desolate sound she could imagine—and she wasn't imagining it.

She set her china teacup onto the coffee table with care, absurdly pleased she hadn't spilled it. She was a country girl now. Country girls didn't get spooked by wolves.

Yes, they did.

She fought for logic. Wolves didn't exist in Banksia Bay. This was the north coast of New South Wales.

Was it a dingo?

Her landlord hadn't mentioned dingoes.

He wouldn't, she thought bitterly. Gabe Carver was one of the most taciturn men she'd ever met. He spoke in monosyllabic grunts. 'Sign here. Rent first Tuesday of the month. Any problems, talk to Joe down at the wharf. He's the handyman. Welcome to Banksia Bay.'

Even his welcome had seemed grudging.

Was he at home?

She peered nervously out into the night and was absurdly comforted to see lights on next door. Actually, it wasn't even next door. This was a huge old house on the headland at the edge of town. Three rooms had been split from the rest of the house and a kitchen installed to make her lovely apartment.

Her landlord was thus right through the wall. They shared the entrance porch. Taciturn or not, the thought that he was at home was reassuring. The burly seaman seemed tough, capable, powerful—even vaguely scary. If the wolf came in...

This was crazy. Nothing was coming in. Her door was locked. And it couldn't be a wolf. It was...

The howl came again, long, low and filling the night with despair.

Despair?

What would she know?

It was just a dog, howling at the moon.

It didn't sound like...just a howl.

She peered out again, then tugged the curtains closed. Logical or not, this was scary. Barricade the door and go to bed. It was the only logical thing to do.

Another howl.

Pain.

Desolation.

Did pain and desolation make any kind of sense?

Step away from the window, Nikkita, she told herself. This is nothing to do with you. This is weird country stuff.

'I'm a country girl.' She said it out loud.

'Um, no,' she corrected herself. 'You're not. You're a city girl who's lived in Banksia Bay for all of three weeks. You ran here because your low-life boss broke your heart. It was a dumb, irrational move. You know nothing about country living.'

But her landlord was right next door. Dogs? Wolves? Whatever it was, he'd be hearing it. He could deal with it himself or he could call Joe.

She was going to bed.

The howl filled the night, echoing round and round the big old house.

There was a dog out there, in trouble.

It was not Gabe's problem. Not.

The howl came again, mournful as death, filling his head with its misery. If Jem had been here she'd be off to investigate.

He missed Jem so much it was as if he'd lost a part of him.

He was settled in his armchair by the fire. Things were as they'd always been, but the place at his feet was empty.

He'd found Jem sixteen years ago, a scrappy, half grown collie, skin and bones. She was attacking a rotting fish on the beach.

He'd lifted her away, half expecting the starved pup to growl or snap, but she'd turned and licked his face with her disgusting tongue—and sealed a friendship for life.

She passed away in her sleep, three months back. He still put his hand down, expecting the warmth of her rough coat. Expecting her to be…there.

The howl cut across his thoughts. Impossible to ignore.

He swore.

Okay, he didn't want to get involved—when had he ever?—but he couldn't bear this. The howl was coming from the beach. If a dog was trapped down there… The tide was on its way in.

Why would a dog be trapped on the beach?

Why would a dog be on the beach?

The howl…again.

He sighed. Abandoned his book. Hauled on the battered sou'wester that, as a professional fisherman, was his second skin. Tugged on his boots and headed for the door.

There wasn't a lot of use staring at the fire anyway. He'd made a conscious decision when his wife walked away to never live with anyone again. Emotional connection spelled disaster.

That didn't mean he had to like his solitary life. With Jem it had been just okay.

Not any more.

Her silk pyjamas were laid out on her pretty pink quilt, waiting for her to climb into her brand new single bed. But the howling went on.

She couldn't bear it.

She might not be a country girl but she'd figured whatever was out there was distressed, not threatening. The howl contained all the misery in the world.

Her landlord lived next door. He should fix it, but would he?

The first day she'd been here she'd worried about pipes gurgling in her antiquated bathroom. The bathroom was vast, the bathtub was huge, and the plumbing looked as if it had come from a medieval castle. The gurgling had her thinking there was no way she was using the bath.

Gabe had been outside, chopping wood. She'd hesitated to approach, intimidated by his gruffness—and also the size, the sense of innate power, the sheer masculinity of the man. Chopping wood… he'd looked quite something.

Actually…he'd been stripped to the waist and he'd looked *really* something.

She was being stupid. Hormonal. Dumb. She'd plucked up courage and approached, feeling like

Oliver Twist asking for more gruel. 'Please sir, could you fix my pipes?'

'See Joe,' he'd muttered and promptly disappeared.

She'd been disconcerted for days.

She'd seethed for a bit, tried to ignore the gurgling for a few days, had showers, and finally gone to find Joe.

Joe was an ancient ex-fisherman living on a dilapidated schooner that looked as if it hadn't been to sea for years. He'd promised to fix the gurgling that afternoon. He did—sort of—thumping the pipes with a spanner—but while she'd been explaining the problem, a fishing boat swept past. Huge. Freshly painted. Gleaming clean and white. The deck was stacked with cray-pots. The superstructure was strung with scores of lanterns that Joe explained were to attract squid.

Her landlord had been at the wheel.

Still disconcerting. Big, weathered, powerful.

Still capable of doing things to her hormones just by…being.

'Turns his hand to anything, that one,' Joe told her as they watched Gabe go past. 'Some of the guys here just fish for squid. Or crays. Or tuna. Then there's a drop in numbers, or sales go off and they're in trouble. I've been a fisherman all my life and I've seen so many go to the wall. Gabe just buys 'em out and keeps going. He went away for a while, but came back when things got bad. Bailed us out. Six of the boats here are his.'

At the wheel of his boat, Gabe looked an imposing figure. His sou'wester might have once been yellow, but that time was long past. He wore oversized waterproof trousers with braces, rubber boots and a faded checked shirt rolled up to reveal arms maybe four times the width of hers. His eyes were creased against the elements, and his face looked almost grim.

After days at sea, his stubble was almost a beard. His thick black hair—in need of a cut—was stiff with salt.

His boat passed within yards of Joe's, and he gave Joe a salute. No smile, though.

He didn't look as if he ever smiled.

He bought up other fishermen when they went broke? He made money out of other people's misery?

Her hormones needed to find someone else to fantasise about, fast.

'I'd guess he's not popular,' she'd ventured, but Joe had looked at her as if she was crazy.

'Are you kidding? Without Gabe, the fishing industry here'd be bust. He buys out the guys who go broke, gives 'em a fair price, then employs 'em to keep working. He's got thirty men and women working for him now, all making a better living than they ever did solo, and there's not one but who'd lay down their lives for him. Not that he'd ask. Never asks anything of anyone. Never lets anyone close. If anyone's in trouble Gabe's first on hand, doing what needs doing, whatever the cost. But he doesn't want thanks. Backs off a mile if you try and give it. He keeps to himself, our Gabe. Apart from that one disaster of a marriage, he always has and he always will. The town respects that. We'd be nuts not to.'

He paused, watching as Gabe expertly manoeuvred his boat into a berth that seemed way too small to take her. He did it as if he was parking a Mini Minor in a paddock, as if he had all the room in the world. 'But now his dog's died,' Joe said slowly, reflectively. 'I dunno… We've never seen him without her; not since he was a lad, and how he's handling it…' He broke off and shook his head. 'Yeah, well, about those pipes…'

That was two weeks ago.

Another howl jerked her back to the present. A dog in trouble.

Desolation?

She had to do something.

There was nothing she could do. This was something her landlord had to cope with.

The howl came again, long, low and dreadful.

She'd tugged on her pyjama top. Almost defiantly.

Another howl.

She paused, torn.

What if her landlord wasn't at home? What if he'd left the light on and was gone?

There was a dog out there in trouble.

Not your problem. NYP. NYP. NYP.

She closed her eyes.

Another howl.

She hauled off her pyjamas and tugged on jeans. Designer jeans. She should do something about her clothes.

She should do something about a dog.

Where was a torch?

What if it was a dingo?

She grabbed her mobile phone. Checked reception. Checked she had the emergency services number on speed dial.

There was a heavy metal poker by the fireside. So far she hadn't lit the fire—or she had once but it had smoked and what did you do about a fire that smoked?

You bought a nice clean electric fire.

Another howl—they were now almost continuous.

Enough.

Poker in one hand, torch in the other, country-girl Nikki—or not—went to see.

The beach beneath the headland was bushland almost to the water's edge. Gabe strode down the darkened track with ease. He'd lived here all his life—he practically knew each twig. He didn't need a torch. In moonlight, torchlight stopped you seeing the big picture.

He reached the beach and looked out to the water's edge. Following the howl.

A huge dog. Skinny. Really skinny. Standing in the shallows, howling with all the misery in the world.

Gabe walked steadily forward, not wanting to startle it, walking as if he was strolling slowly along the beach and hadn't even noticed the dog.

The dog saw him. It stopped howling and backed further into the water. Obviously terrified.

A wolfhound? A wolfhound mixed with something else. Black and shaggy and desolate.

'It's okay.' He was still twenty yards away. 'Hey, boy, it's fine. You going to tell me what's the matter?'

The dog stilled.

It was seriously big. And seriously skinny. And very, very wet.

Had it come off a boat?

He thought suddenly of Jem, shivering on the beach sixteen years back. Jem, breaking his heart.

This dog was nothing to do with him. *This was not another Jem.*

He couldn't leave it, though. Could he entice it up the cliff? If he could get it into his truck he'd take it to Henrietta who ran t. shelter.

That was the extent of his broke your heart almost worse tha. ~~ent. Dogs~~

'I'm not going to hurt you.' He'e. brought some steak, something to coax'd have want to come home and get a feed? Here, bo;' 'You

The dog backed still further. For whatever reason, this dog didn't want company. He looked a great ga-lumphing frame of terror.

It'd have to be steak. There was no way he'd catch him without.

'Stay here,' he told the dog. 'Two minutes tops and I'll be back with supper. You like rump steak?'

The dog was almost haunch-deep in water. Was he dumb or just past acting rationally?

'Two minutes,' he promised. 'Don't go away.'

The dog was on the beach. As soon as she walked out of the front door she figured it out. The house was on the headland and the howls were echoing straight up.

Should she knock on her landlord's side of the house?

If he was home he must be hearing this, she thought, and if he'd heard it and done nothing, then no amount of pleading would make a difference. Jo said he helped people. Ha!

eard and decided to ignore it. He

He m d, a loner.

was lik see?

Kn s worse, the Hound of the Baskervilles

W dlord?

or h t be stupid. Knock.

e knocked.

Nothing.

She didn't know whether to be relieved or not.

Another howl.

What next? Ring the police?

What would she say? Excuse me but there's a dog on the beach. What sort of wimpy statement was that?

She needed to see what was happening.

Cautiously.

There was a narrow track from the house to the beach but she'd only been on it a couple of times. It was a private track, practically overgrown. Where did the track start?

She searched the edge of the overgrown garden with the torch but she couldn't find it.

So was she going to bush-bash her way down to the cove?

This was nuts. Dangerous nuts.

Only it wasn't dangerous. There was only about fifty yards of bush-land between the house and the beach. The bush wasn't so thick she couldn't push through.

And that howl was doing things to her insides. It

sounded like she imagined the Hound of the Basker-villes would sound, howling ghostly anguish over the moors. Or over her beach.

The animal must be stuck in a trap or something.

If it was stuck, what could she do?

Go to the beach, figure what's wrong and then ring for help.

You can do this. You're a big girl. A country girl. Or not.

She wanted, suddenly and desperately, to be back home in Sydney. In her lovely life she'd walked away from.

Face that tomorrow, she told herself harshly. For tonight…go fix a howl.

He was striding up the track, moving swiftly. With a slab of meat in his hand he could approach the dog slowly, letting it smell the meat before it smelled him. He'd intended to have the steak for break-fast—he needed a decent meal before heading to sea again—but he could cope with eggs.

Don't get sucked in.

'I'm not getting sucked in,' he told himself. 'I'm hauling the thing out of the water, feeding it and handing it over to Henrietta. End of story.'

It was dark.

The bush was really thick. Her torch wasn't strong enough.

She was out of her mind.

The howls stopped.

Why?

The silence made it worse. Where had the howls been coming from? Where were the howls now?

Anything could be in here. Bunyips. Neanderthals. The odd rapist.

She was losing her mind, and she was going home now! She turned, pushed forward, and a branch slapped her forehead with a swish of leaves. She almost screamed. She was absurdly pleased that she didn't.

But still no howl.

Where was it?

She was going back to the house. There was no way she was going one inch further.

Where was the thing behind the howl?

She shoved her way around the next bush, pushing herself against the thick foliage. Suddenly the foliage gave way and she almost tumbled out onto the track.

Hands grabbed her shoulders—and held.

She screamed and jerked back.

She raised her poker and she hit.

CHAPTER TWO

SHE'D killed him.

He went down like felled timber, crumpling from the knees, pitching sideways onto the leaf-littered track.

She had just enough courage not to run; to shine the torch at what she'd hit.

She'd hit someone—not something. She didn't believe in werewolves. Therefore...

Sanity returned with terrifying speed. She had it figured almost before she got the torchlight on his face, and what she saw confirmed it.

She whimpered. There seemed no other option.

This was ghastly on so many levels her head felt it might explode.

She'd knocked out her landlord.

The howling started up again just through the trees, and she jumped higher than the first time she'd heard it.

A lesser woman would run.

There wasn't room for her to be a lesser woman.

She knelt, shining the torchlight closer to see the damage.

Gabe's dark face was thick with stubble, harsh and angular. A thin trickle of blood was oozing down the side of his cheek. A bruise with a split at its centre was rising above his eye.

He seemed totally unconscious.

To say her heart sank was an understatement. Her heart was below her ankles. It was threatening to abandon her body entirely.

But then… He stirred and groaned and his fingers moved towards his head.

Conscious. That had to be good.

What to do? Deep breath. This was no time for hysterics. He looked as if he was trying to focus.

She placed the poker behind her. Out of sight.

'Are you… Are you okay?' she managed.

He groaned. He closed his eyes and appeared to think about it.

'No,' he managed at last. 'I'm not.'

'I'll find a doctor.' Her voice wobbled to the point of ridiculous. 'An ambulance.'

He opened his eyes again, touched his head, winced, closed his eyes again. 'No.'

'You need help.' She was gabbling. 'Someone.' She went to touch his face and then thought better of it. She definitely needed help. Someone who knew what they were doing. She reached inside her jacket for her cellphone.

His eyes flew open, he grabbed her wrist and he held like a vice.

'What did you hit me with?' His voice was a slurred growl.

'A…a poker.' His voice was deep. In contrast, her voice was practically a squeak.

'A poker,' he said, almost conversationally. 'Of course. And now what?'

'S…sorry?'

'You have a gun in your jacket? Or is only your poker loaded?'

Her breath came out in a rush. If he was making stupid jokes, maybe she hadn't done deathly damage.

'There's not…that's not funny,' she managed. 'You scared the daylights out of me.'

'You *hit* the daylights out of me.'

Reaction was making her shake. 'You snuck up.' Her voice was getting higher. 'You grabbed me.'

'Snuck up…' He sounded flabbergasted. 'I believe,' he said through gritted teeth, 'that I was running up the track. On *my* land. Back to *my* house. And you burst out of the undergrowth. Bearing poker.'

He had a point, she conceded. She'd almost fallen as she lurched onto the cleared track. She might indeed have fallen into his path.

It might even have been reasonable for him to grab her to stop them both falling.

And he was her landlord. Hitting someone was bad enough, but to hit Gabe...

It hadn't been easy to find decent rental accommodation in Banksia Bay and she'd been really lucky to find this apartment. Apart from howling dogs, it had everything she needed. 'Just be nice to your landlord and respect his privacy,' the woman in the rental agency had advised. 'He's a bit of a loner. You leave Gabe in peace and you'll get along fine.'

Leaving him in peace wouldn't include hitting him, she conceded. Mentally she was already packing.

'I need steak,' he said across her thoughts.

She blinked. 'Steak?' She groped for basic first aid; thought of something she'd once read. 'To stop the swelling?' She tried to look wise. Tried to stop gibbering. 'I don't... I don't have steak but I'll get ice.'

'For the dog, dummy.' He'd raised his head but now he set it down again, staying flat on the leaf litter. Gingerly fingering the bruise. 'The dog needs help. There's steak in my fridge. Fetch it.'

'I can't...'

'Just fetch it,' he snapped and closed his eyes. 'If you run round in the middle of the night with pokers, you face the consequences. Get the steak.'

'I can't leave you,' she said miserably, and he opened one eye and looked at her. Flinching.

'Turn the torch around,' he said, and she realised

that just possibly she was blinding him as well as hitting him.

'Sorry.' She swivelled the light so it was shining harmlessly into the bush.

'No, onto you.'

He reached out, grabbed the flashlight and turned it onto her face. Then he surveyed her while she thought ouch, having a flashlight in her eyes hurt.

'There's no need to be scared,' he said.

'I'm not scared.' But then the dog howled again and she jumped. Okay, maybe she was.

'You can't afford to be,' he said, and she could tell by the strain in his voice that he was hurting. 'Because the dog needs help. I don't know what's wrong with him. He's standing on the beach howling. You were heading down with a poker. I, on the other hand, intend to try steak. I believe my method is more humane. It might take me a few moments to stop seeing stars, however, so you fetch it.'

'Are you really seeing stars?'

'Yes.' Then he relented. 'It's night. There are stars. Yes, I'm dizzy, but I'll get over it. I won't die while you're away, but I do need a minute to stop things spinning. My door's open. Kitchen's at the back. Steak's in the paper parcel in the fridge. Chop it into bite sized pieces. I'll lie here and count stars till you come back. Real ones.'

'I can't leave you. I need to call for help.'

'I'm fine,' he said with exaggerated patience. 'I've

had worse bumps than this and lived. Just do what I ask like a good girl and give me space to recover.'

'You lost consciousness. I can't…'

'If I did it was momentary and I don't need anyone to hold my hand,' he snapped. 'Neither do you. You're wasting time, woman. Go.'

She went. Feeling dreadful.

She tracked the path with her torch, trying to run. She couldn't. The path was a mass of tree roots. If Gabe had been running he must know the path by heart.

She didn't have the right shoes for running either.

She didn't have the right shoes at all, she thought. She was wearing Gucci loafers. They worked beautifully for wandering the Botanic Gardens in Sydney after a Sunday morning latte. They didn't work so well here.

She wanted so much to be back in her lovely apartment overlooking Sydney Harbour. Back in her beautifully contained life, her wonderful job, her friends, the lovely parties, the coffee haunts, control.

Jon's fabulous apartment. A job in a lovely office right next to Jon's. A career that paid…extraordinarily. A career with Jon. Friends she shared with Jon. Coffee haunts where people greeted Jon before they greeted her.

Jon's life. Or half of Jon's life. She'd thought she had the perfect life and it had been based on a lie.

What to do when your world crumbled?

Run. She'd run to here.

'Don't think about it.' She said it to herself as a mantra, over and over, as she headed up the track as fast as she could in her stupid shoes. There'd been enough self-pity. This was her new life. Wandering around in the dark, coshing her landlord, looking for steak for the Hound of the Baskervilles?

It was her new life until tomorrow, she thought miserably. Tomorrow Gabe would ask her to leave.

Another city might be more sensible than moving back to Sydney. But it was probably time she faced the fact that moving to the coast had been a romantic notion, a dignified way she could explain her escape to friends.

'I can't stand the rat race any longer. I can deal with my clients through the Internet and the occasional city visit. I see myself in a lovely little house overlooking the sea, just me and my work and time to think.'

Her friends—Jon's friends—thought she was nuts, but then they didn't know the truth about Jon.

Scumbag.

She'd walked away from a scumbag. Now she'd hit her landlord.

Men! Where was a nice convent when a girl

needed one? A cloistered convent where no man set foot. Ever.

There seemed to be a dearth of convents on her way back to the house.

Steak.

She reached the house, and headed through the porch they shared, where two opposite doors delineated His and Hers.

She'd never been in His. She opened his door cautiously as if there might be a Hound or two in there as well.

No Hounds. The sitting room looked old and faded and comfy, warmed by a gorgeous open fire. There was one big armchair by the fire. A half-empty beer glass. Books scattered—lots of books. Masculine, unfussed, messy.

All this she saw at a glance as she headed towards the kitchen, but strangely…here was the hormone thing again. She was distracted by the sheer masculinity of the place.

As she was…distracted…by the sheer masculinity of her landlord.

Stupid. Get on with it, she told herself crossly, and she did.

His fridge held more than hers. Meat, vegetables, fruit, sauces—interesting stuff that said when he was at home he cooked.

She needed to learn, she thought suddenly, as she caught the whiff of meals past and glanced at the big old firestove that was the centrepiece of the kitchen. Enough with 'Waistline Cuisine'.

It was hardly the time to be thinking cooking classes now, though. Or hormones.

Steak.

She had it. A solid lump, enough for a team of Hounds. She sliced it into chunks in seconds, then opened the freezer and grabbed a packet of frozen peas as well.

First aid and Hound meat, coming up.

Men and dogs. She could cope.

She had no choice. Convents had to wait.

What did you do with hormones in convents?

He'd terrified her.

Gabe lay back and looked at the sky and let his head clear. She'd packed a huge punch, but any anger he felt had been wiped by the look on her face. She'd looked sicker than he felt.

What was he about, letting the place to a needy city woman?

It was the second time he'd let it. The first time he'd rented it to Mavis, a spinster with two dogs. The moment she'd moved in she decided he needed mothering. Finally, after six months of tuna bakes, her mother had 'a turn' and Mavis headed back to Sydney to take care of her. Gabe had been so relieved he'd waived the last month's rent.

And now this.

Dorothy in the letting agency had made this woman sound businesslike and sensible. Very different to Mavis.

'Nikkita Morrissy. Thirty years old. She designs air conditioning systems for big industrial projects. Her usual schedule is three weeks home, one week on site, often overseas. She's looking for a quiet place with a view, lots of natural light and nothing to disturb her.'

A woman who worked in industrial engineering. She sounded clever, efficient and non-needy.

His house was huge. He should move into town but he'd lived in this place all his life. *His mother was here*.

He'd lost his mother when he was eight years old, and this was all that was left. The garden she'd loved. The fence she'd almost finished. He walked outside sometimes and he could swear he saw her.

'I'll never leave you...'

People lied. He'd learned that early. Depend on no one. But here…in his mother's garden, looking out over the bay she'd loved, this was all that was left of a promise he'd desperately wanted to believe in.

Emotional nonsense? Of course it was, he knew it, but his childhood house was a good place to crash when he wasn't at sea. He had the money to keep it. If he could get a reasonable tenant for the apartment, then there'd be someone keeping the rooms warm, used.

Go ahead, he'd told Dorothy.

And then he'd met Nikkita. Briefly, the day she'd moved in.

She didn't look like an industrial engineer. She looked like someone in one of those glossy magazines Hattie kept leaving on the boat. She was tall, five nine or so, slim and pale-skinned, with huge eyes and professionally applied make-up—yes, he was a bachelor but that didn't mean he couldn't pick decent cosmetics a mile off. Her glossy black hair was cut into some sort of sculpted bob, dead straight, all fringe and sharp edges.

And her clothes… The day she'd arrived she'd been wearing a black tunic with a diagonal slash of crimson across the hips. She'd added loopy silver earrings, red tights and glossy black boots that were practically thigh high. Low heels though. It was her moving day. She'd obviously thought low heels were workmanlike.

Tonight she'd been wearing jeans. Skin-tight jeans and a soft pink sweater. She must be roughing it, he thought, and his thoughts were bitter.

His head was thumping. He was trying hard not to think critical thoughts about ditzy air conditioning engineers who bush-bashed through the night with pokers.

And suddenly she was back again—practically

running, though if she'd tried to run in those shoes
she would have run right out of them. She was pant-
ing. Her eyes were still huge and the sculpted hair
was...well, a lot less sculpted. She had a twig stuck
behind one ear. A big twig.

'Are you okay?' she demanded, breathless, as if
she'd expected to find him dead.

'I'm fine,' he growled and struggled to stand.
Enough of lying round feeling sorry for himself.
He shook away the hand she proffered, pushed himself to his feet—and the world swayed. Not much,
but enough for him to grab her hand to steady himself.

She was stronger than he thought. She grabbed
his other hand and held, hard, waiting for him to
steady.

'S...sorry.' For a moment he thought he might
throw up. He concentrated for a bit and decided no,
he might keep his dignity.

'Let me help you to the house.'

'Dog first,' he said.

'You first.'

'The dog's standing up to his hocks in the water,
howling. I'm not even whinging. I'm prioritizing.'
He made to haul his hands away but she still held.

He stopped pulling and let her hold.

Two reasons. One, he was still unsteady.

Two, it felt...not bad at all.

He worked with women. A good proportion of

his fishing crews were female. They mostly smelled of, yeah, well, of fish. After a while, no matter how much washing, you didn't get the smell out.

Nikkita smelled of something citrussy and tangy and outright heady. It didn't make the dizziness worse, though. In truth it helped. He stood still, breathing in the scent of her, while the night settled around him.

She didn't speak. She simply held.

Two minutes. Three. She wasn't a talker, then. She'd figured he needed time to make the ground solid and she was giving it to him. It was the first decent thing he'd seen of her.

Maybe there were more decent things.

Her hands felt good. They were small hands for a tall woman. Soft…

Yeah, well, of course they'd be soft. For the last ten years any woman he'd ever gone out with was a local, one of the fishing crews, women who worked hard for a living. The only woman he'd ever gone out with who had soft hands…

Yeah. Lisbette. He'd married her.

So much for soft hands.

'I'm right now,' he said, finally, as another howl split the night. 'Dog.'

'Please let me take you home first.'

'Are you good with dogs?'

'Um…no.'

'Then we both do the dog,' he said. 'Sure, I'm unsteady, so you do what I tell you. Exactly what I tell you. After the poker, it's the least you can do.'

Was she out of her mind?

She was acting under orders.

Gabe was sitting in the shadows, watching, as she approached the dog with her hands full of steak. Up-wind, according to Gabe's directions, so he could smell the meat.

The dog was huge. Soaking wet, its coat was clinging to its skinny frame, so it looked almost like a small black horse.

Talk gently, Gabe had said. Soft, unthreatening.

So... 'Hey, Horse, it's okay,' she told him. 'Come out of the water and have some steak. Gabe's gone to a lot of trouble to get it for you. The least you can do is eat it.'

Take one small step after another, Gabe had told her. Stop at the first hint of nervousness. Let the dog figure for himself that you're not a threat.

'Come on, boy. Hey, Horse, it's okay. It's fine. Come and tell me what your real name is.'

What was she doing, standing in the shallows with her hands full of raw meat? She'd tugged off her shoes but her jeans were soaked. To no avail. The dog was backing away, still twenty feet from her.

His coat was ragged, long and dripping. Fur was matted over his eyes.

He wasn't coming near.

If Gabe wasn't in the shadows watching she might have set the meat down on the sand and retreated.

But her landlord was expecting her to do this. He'd do it himself, only, despite what he told her, the thump on the head was making him nauseous. She knew it. He wasn't letting her call for help but she knew it went against the grain to let her approach the dog. Especially when she was so bad at it.

'Here, Horse. Here…'

A wave, bigger than the rest, came sideways instead of forward. It slapped into another wave, crested, hit her fair across the chest.

She yelped. She couldn't help herself.

The dog backed fast into the waves.

'It's okay,' she called and forgot to lower her voice.

The dog cast her a terrified glance and backed some more. The next wave knocked him sideways. He regained his footing and ran, like the horse he resembled. Along the line of the surf, away, around the bed in the headland and out of sight.

'It's okay.'

It wasn't, but she hadn't expected him to say it. She'd expected him to yell.

She'd coshed him. She'd scared the dog away.

A little voice at the back of her mind was saying, *At least the howling's stopped.*

NYP, the same little voice in the back of her

head whispered. Not your problem. She could forget the dog.

Only... He'd looked tragic. Horse...

Gabe was sitting where the sand gave way to the grassy verge before the bush began. At least he looked okay. At least he was still conscious.

'You did the best you could.' *For a city girl.* It wasn't said. It didn't have to be said.

'Maybe he's gone home.'

'Does he look to you like he has a home?' He flicked his cellphone from his top pocket and punched in numbers. Then he glanced at her, sighed, and hit loudspeaker so she could hear who he was talking to.

A male voice. Authoritive. 'Banksia Bay Police,' the voice said.

'Raff?' Gabe's voice still wasn't completely steady and the policeman at the end of the line obviously heard it. Maybe he was used to people with unsteady voices calling. He also recognised the caller.

'Gabe? What's up?' She heard concern.

'No problem. Or not a major one. A stray dog.'

'Another one.' The policeman sighed.

'What are you talking about?' Gabe demanded.

'Henrietta's Animal Welfare van was involved in an accident a few days back,' the policeman explained. 'We have stray dogs all over town. Describe this one.'

'Big, black and malnourished,' Gabe said. He was

watching Nikki as he spoke. Nikki was trying to get the sand from between her toes before she put her shoes on. It wasn't working.

She was soaking. She sat and the sand stuck to her. Ugh.

She was also unashamedly listening.

'Like Great Dane big?'

'Yeah, but he's shaggy,' Gabe said. 'I'd guess Wolfhound with a few other breeds mixed in as well. And I don't have him. He was down the beach below the house. We tried to catch him with a lump of steak but he's headed round the headland to your side of town.'

'We?' Raff said.

'Yeah,' Gabe said dryly. 'My tenant's been helpful.'

'But the two of you can't catch him.'

'No,' Gabe said, and Nikki thought miserably that he sounded as if he could have done it if he was by himself. Maybe he could, but at least he didn't say so.

'I'll check from the headland in the morning,' Raff was saying. 'You okay? You sound odd.'

'Nothing I can't handle. If he comes back…you want me to take him to the shelter?'

'You might as well take him straight to the vet's,' Raff said. 'He was on his way there to be put down. If he's the one I think he is, someone threw him off a boat a couple of weeks back. We found him on the beach, starving. He's well past cute pup stage. He's huge and shabby. Old scars and not a lot of loveliness. He looks like he's been kicked and neglected. No one will rehouse a dog like that, so Henrietta made the decision to get him put down. But if he doesn't come back to your beach it's not your worry, mate. Thanks for letting me know. 'Night.'

''Night.'

Gabe repocketed his phone.

Nikki flicked more sand away.

A starving dog. Kicked and neglected. Thrown from a boat. She hadn't even managed to give him a meal, and now he was lost again.

Plus a landlord who was still sounding shaken because she'd thumped him.

Was there a scale for feeling bad? Bad, terrible, appalling.

'Leave the steak just above the high tide mark,' Gabe said, his voice gentle. 'It's not your fault.'

'Nice of you to say so.'

'Yeah, well, the bang on the head was your fault,' he conceded, and he even managed a wry smile. 'But there's nothing more we can do for the dog. He's gone. If he smelled the steak he might come back, but he won't come near if he smells us. We've done all we can. Moving on, I need an aspirin. Do you have those toes sand-free yet?'

'I…yes.' No. She was crusted in sand but she stood up and prepared to move on.

She glanced along the beach, half hoping the dog would lope back.

Why would he?

'Raff'll find him,' Gabe said.

'He's the local cop?'

'Yes.'

'He won't look tonight?'

'There's no hope of finding him tonight. The beach around the headland is inaccessible at high tide. We'll find him tomorrow.'

'You'll look, too?'

'I'm leaving at dawn,' he said. 'I have fish to catch, but you're welcome to look all you want. Now, if you want to stay here you're also welcome, but I need my bed.'

She followed him up the track, feeling desolate. But Gabe must be feeling worse than she was. Maybe he was walking slowly to cater for her lack of sensible shoes, but she didn't think so. Once he stumbled and she put out a hand. He steadied, looked down at her hand and shook his head. And winced again.

'I hit you hard,' she muttered.

'Women aren't what they used to be,' he said. 'Whatever happened to a nice, tidy slap across the cheek? That's what they do in movies.'

'I'll remember it next time.'

'There won't be a next time,' he said, and she thought uh-oh, was her tenancy on the line?

'I'm not about to evict you,' he said wearily, and she flinched. Beside being clumsy and stupid, was she also transparent?

'I didn't think...'

'That I was about to evict you for hitting me? Good.'

'Thank you,' she said feebly and he went on concentrating on putting one foot in front of the other.

He didn't stop until they reached the house. The lights were still on. He stood back to let her precede him into the porch. Instead of going straight into her side of the house, she paused.

Under the porch-light he looked...ill. Yes, he still looked large, dark and dangerous, but he also looked pale under the weathering, and the thin trickle of blood was at the centre of a bruise that promised to be ugly.

He staggered a bit. She reached out instinctively but he grabbed the veranda post. Steadied.

She could have killed him. He looked so...so...

Male?

There was a sensible thought.

'You could have me arrested,' she managed. 'I'm so sorry.'

'But you weren't planning to hit the dog.' It wasn't a question.

'N...no.'

'That's why I won't have you arrested. You meant well.'

'You need to see a doctor.'

'I need to go to bed.'

'But what if it's terrible?' she said before she could stop herself. 'I've read about head wounds. People get hit on the head and go to bed and never wake up. You should get your pupils looked at. If one's bigger than the other…or is it if one doesn't move? I don't know, but I do know that you should get yourself checked. Please, can I drive you to the hospital?'

'No.' Flat. Inflexible. Non negotiable.

'Why not?'

'I've spent my life on boats. Believe it or not, I've been thumped a lot worse than this. I'm fine.'

'You should be checked.'

'You want to look at my pupils?'

'I wouldn't know what to look for. But if you go to bed now… It could be dangerous. Please…'

He was too close, she thought. He was too big. He smelled of the sea. But maybe it wasn't just the sea. He smelled of diesel oil, and fish, and salt, and other incredibly masculine smells she'd never smelled before.

The only man she'd been this close to in the last few years was Jon. Jon of the sleek business suits, of expensive aftershave, of cool, sleek, corporate style.

Compared to Jon, Gabe was another species. They both might be guys at the core, but externally Gabe had been left behind in the cave. Or at sea.

Beside Gabe she felt small and insignificant and stupid. And he made her feel…vulnerable? Maybe, but something more. Exposed. It was a feeling she couldn't explain and she didn't want to explain. All she knew was that she didn't want to be beside him one moment longer, but she was still worried about him. That worry wouldn't be ignored.

'You should be checked every couple of hours,' she said, doggedly now. Once upon a time, well before Jon, she'd dated a medical student. She knew this much.

'I'm fine.' He was getting irritated. 'In eight hours I'll be out at sea. I need to go to bed now. Goodnight.'

'At least let me check.'

'Check what?'

'Check you. All night.'

He stilled. They were far too close. The porch was far too small. Exposed? It was a dumb thought, but that was definitely how he made her feel. His face was lined, worn, craggy. He couldn't be much over thirty, she thought, but he looked as if life had been hard.

It could get harder if she didn't check him. If he was to die…

'What are you talking about?' he demanded.

'I need to check you every two hours,' she said miserably, knowing her conscience would let her off with nothing less. 'I'll come in and make sure you're conscious.'

'I won't be conscious. I'll be asleep.'

'Then I'll wake you and you can tell me your name and what day it is and then you can go back to sleep.'

'I won't know which day it is.'

'Then tell me how much you dislike the tenant next door,' she said, starting to feel desperate. 'For worrying. But I need to do this.' Deep breath. 'It's two-hour checks or I'll phone your friend, the cop, and I tell him how badly I hit you. I wouldn't be the least bit surprised if he's the kind of guy who'll be up here with sirens blazing making you see sense.'

Silence.

Her guess was right, she thought. In that one short phone conversation she'd sensed friendship between the two men, and maybe the unknown cop was as tough as the guy standing in front of her.

'I'm serious,' she said, jutting her jaw.

'I'll be on the boat at dawn. This is nonsense.'

'Being on the boat at dawn is nonsense. After a hit like that you should stay home.'

'Butt out of my life!' It was an explosion and she backed as far as the little porch allowed. Which wasn't far, but something must have shown in her face.

'Okay, sorry.' He raked his hand through his thatch of dark, unruly hair. He needed a haircut,

Nikki thought inconsequentially. And then she thought, even more inconsequentially, what would he look like in a suit?

Like a caged tiger. This guy was not meant to be constrained.

That was what she was doing now, she thought. She was constraining him, but she wasn't backing down. There was no way she could calmly go to bed and leave him to die next door.

She met his gaze and jutted her chin some more and tried to look determined. She was determined.

'Every two hours or Raff,' she said.

'Fine.' He threw up his hands in defeat. 'Have it your way. You can sleep tomorrow; I can't. I'm going to bed. If you shine your torch in my eyes every two hours I might well tell you what I think of you.'

'Fine by me,' she said evenly. 'As long as you're alive.'

'Goodnight,' he snapped and turned away. But as he did she saw him wince again.

She really had hurt him.

She showered and tried not to think about dead landlords and starving dogs. What else?

Live landlords. Two-hourly checks. Pupil dilation?

Maybe not. Questions would have to do.

Her pipes gurgled.

She thought briefly about discussing antiquated

pipes every two hours but decided, on balance, maybe not. Name and date. Keep it formal and brief.

She set her alarm for two hours on but she didn't sleep. Two hours later she tiptoed in next door.

She'd forgotten to ask which was his bedroom. It was a huge house.

There was a note on the floor in the passage, with an arrow pointing to the left.

'Florence Nightingale, this way.'

She managed a smile. Her first smile of the night. Okay, he'd accepted her help.

She tiptoed in.

He was sprawled on a big bed, the covers only to his waist. Face down, arms akimbo.

Bare back. Very bare back.

She was using her torch. She should quickly focus on his head, wake him, make sure he was coherent, then slip away.

Instead, she took just a moment to check out that body.

Wow.

Double wow.

His shoulders were twice the size of Jon's, but there was no hint of fat. This was pure muscle. A lifetime of pulling in nets, of hauling cray-pots, of hard manual labour, had tuned his body to...

Perfection.

It wasn't often that Nikki let herself look at a guy and think sheer physical perfection but she did now.

The weathering of the man…a life on the sea…

There was a scar on his shoulder, thin and white. She wanted, quite suddenly, to reach out and trace…

'I'm alive,' he snapped. 'Gabriel Carver, Tuesday the fourteenth. Go away.'

She almost yelped again. Habit-forming?

'Your…your head's hurting?'

'Not if I close my eyes and think of England. Instead of thinking of women with pokers. Go away.'

She went.

At least he was alive.

And at least she hadn't touched him. She hadn't traced that scar.

She still wanted to.

Nonsense.

She didn't sleep for another two hours. She checked again. He was sprawled on his back. He looked as if he'd been fighting with the bed.

He was deeply asleep this time, but he looked… done. The bruise on his face looked awful.

She couldn't see the scar on his back. All she could see was his face, exhaustion—pain?

Something inside her twisted. A giant of a man.

Just a little bit vulnerable?

He wouldn't thank her for thinking it but, stupid or not, the thought was there.

It was two in the morning. She glanced at his bedside clock. His alarm was set for four.

She hesitated. Then, carefully, she removed the

clock, flicked the alarm off and slipped it in her pocket. His phone was on the bedside table. Why not go all the way? She pocketed that, too.

Then she touched his face. The good side.

His eyes opened. He looked a bit dazed, but he did focus. This was nothing more than someone waking from deep sleep.

'I'll live,' he said, slurred.

'Say something bitter.'

'I'm removing all fireside implements from rental properties.'

'That'll do,' she said and let him go back to sleep.

At four she checked him again. Another slurred response but just as together. Excellent. One more check would get her in the clear, she thought. No more inspections of semi-naked landlords.

She wasn't sure whether to be glad or sorry.

Glad, she told herself, astounded where her thoughts were taking her. Of course, glad.

She went back to bed. Tried not to think of half naked landlords.

Didn't succeed.

At five-thirty Gabe's phone rang. She was on her side of the wall with Gabe's phone beside her bed. She answered. A woman's voice. 'Gabe? Where are you?'

'Hi,' she said cautiously. 'This is Nikki, Gabe's next door neighbour.'

'The city chick,' the woman said blankly.

'That's me.'

'Where's Gabe?'

'I'm sorry, but Gabe had a bit of an accident last night. He won't be in this morning.'

'He won't be in…'

'He can't come to work.'

'What sort of an accident?'

'He fell. He almost knocked himself out. He's got a headache and a badly bruised face.' No need to mention he had the bruised face before he fell.

'Gabe turns up for work when he's half dead.' The woman sounded stunned. 'How bad is he?'

'Determined to come in but I've taken his alarm and his phone and he hasn't woken up.'

There was a moment's awed silence. Then… 'Well, good for you, love. You've got him in bed, you keep him there. When he wakes up, tell him Frank's rung in and his head cold's worse, so it would have only been me on board with him. The *Mariette*'s short a crew member as well, so I'll go on the *Mariette* and the *Lady Nell* can stay in port. That'll play into your hands as well. He no longer has a crew. You keep him in bed with my blessings, for as long as you want. Go for it, girl.'

She disconnected. Laughing.

Nikki stared at the phone as if it stung.

This was a small town. This'd be all over town in minutes.

How would Gabe react?

Um…what had she done?

Whatever. It was done now. She had an hour before the next check.

She really was incredibly tired.

She put her head on her pillow and closed her eyes.

She forgot to set the alarm.

Gabe woke and sunshine was flooding his bedroom. This on its own was a novelty. If the weather was decent he was out fishing, as simple as that.

He opened one eye and tried to figure it out. Why the sunbeams?

His head hurt a bit, not too much, just a dull ache. If he lay still and only opened the one eye it didn't hurt at all.

The sun was streaming through his window. He felt…

Suddenly wide awake. He turned to the bedside table, looking for his clock in disbelief.

No clock.

He groped for his phone.

No phone.

What the…?

His watch.

It was eight o'clock. Eight! He'd slept for ten hours.

The boat. The crew. They'd be waiting.

Where were his…?

Nikkita.

Hitting him on the head was one thing; making him miss a day's fishing was another. She was so out of here.

He threw back the covers and headed for the door, thumping the wall as he went, just to make sure she was awake.

Anger didn't begin to describe what he was feeling. Women!

The thump on her bedroom wall was loud enough to wake the dead. She sat bolt upright. Stared at the clock.

Uh-oh. Uh-oh, uh-oh, uh-oh.

Eight o'clock. She might just have slept in.

She'd missed a check.

At least he wasn't dead, she thought. He should be grateful.

By the sound of the thump on her wall, he wasn't grateful.

By the sound of the thump, he wished for her undivided attention.

Her door was locked. A lesser woman might have tugged the duvet over her head and stayed where she was.

There were a lot of things a lesser woman might do. After today she was going right back to being a lesser woman, but right now…

There wasn't a lot of choice.

She grabbed her robe and headed next door to face Gabe.

She opened her door right as he opened his.

The dog was lying right across the porch.

Her Hound of the Baskervilles.

Horse.

CHAPTER THREE

NIKKI almost tripped and so did Gabe. They were focused on each other. Gabe's face was dark with anger, and Nikki was just plain terrified. Gabe was still only wearing boxers and that didn't help. Neither was looking at their feet and the dog was sprawled like a great wet floor mat.

Both of them stumbled and both had to grab the door jambs to keep their balance.

Both stared down in amazement.

The dog was even bigger than Nikki had thought last night. Four feet high? It was impossible to tell. All she knew was that, prone, he practically covered the small porch.

He was almost as flat as a doormat. He lay motionless, only the faint rise of his chest wall telling her he was alive.

'It's Horse,' she said blankly.

The big dog stirred at her voice. He hauled his great head off the floor, as if making a Herculean effort. He gazed up at her and all the misery of the world was in that gaze. It was a 'kill me now' look.

She didn't know a thing about dogs. If she'd been asked, she'd confess she probably didn't like them much. But that look...

Her heart twisted. In the face of that look, she forgot her landlord and she sank to her knees. 'Oh, my... Oh, Horse...'

'What do you think you're playing at?' Her landlord's voice was like a whip above her. 'You've brought him in here...'

She wasn't listening. The big dog was so wet he couldn't get any wetter. While she watched, a shudder ran though his big frame and she thought...she thought...

She had to help. There was no way she could walk away. Not your problem? Ha.

'Hey, it's okay.' She ignored Gabe. She could only focus on the dog. She could only think about the dog.

'You caught him.' Gabe's voice had lost its edge as he took in Horse's condition.

'I didn't catch him. Maybe he found the meat and followed our scent. Pushed into the porch. Do you think he wants more?'

'Has he been here all night?'

'Are you nuts? Look at him. He's soaking. Why doesn't he move? Should we take him to the vet? Will you help me carry him to the car?'

'Fred will put him down,' Gable said bluntly.

'Fred?'

'The vet.'

That brought her up short. Last night's phone conversation was suddenly replaying in her head.

This dog had been on his way to be put down when he'd escaped. If they took him to the vet, that was what would happen.

'No,' she said. It was all she could think of to say.

'Do you want a dog?'

'I...'

She swallowed. Did she want a dog?

She didn't. She couldn't. But she wasn't thinking past now.

'I'll think about that later,' she said. 'He's not going anywhere until he's dry and warm and fed. Can you help me take him into my place?' She looked up at Gabe, and then she thought...

Anger. Uh-oh.

Maybe there were a few unresolved issues to be addressed before he'd help her.

She was aware again of his body. That chest. Those shoulders.

Hormones.

Anger.

'I slept,' he said, carefully neutral. 'Through my alarm. That might be because it was moved from my bedside table.'

'I slept through it too,' she confessed. 'That's because I forgot to set it.'

'My crew…'

Act efficient, she decided. Brisk. As if she knew what she was doing. 'Hattie's on the…let me think… on the *Mariette*,' she told him. 'Because they're short a crew member. Frank called in sick so the *Lady Nell*'s staying in port. You have the day off.'

He didn't answer. He looked speechless.

'So can you help me with the dog?' she asked.

'You took my alarm.'

'You were sick. I thought I'd killed you. It was the least I could do.'

'You took my phone.'

'Yes, and I talked to Hattie. She agrees you need a day off.'

'It's not her business. It's not your business.'

'No,' she snapped. 'And neither is this dog but he's freezing. Get over it and help me.'

Her gaze locked with his. She could feel his anger, his frustration, his shock.

His body…

His body was almost enough to distract her from his anger, his frustration, his shock.

But she couldn't think of it now. She had the dog to think of. And, while she was chiding herself, Gabe stooped and touched the dog's face.

The dog tried to raise his head again. Failed.

'Don't think you've heard the last of this,' he said grimly. 'But this guy's done.'

'Done.' Nikki cringed. 'He's not dying.'

'Close to.' He'd moved on, she thought. All his attention was now on the dog. He seemed hesitant, as if he didn't want involvement, but the dog stirred and moaned, and something in Gabe's face changed. 'All right,' he said. 'If you're serious, let's get him into my place. The fire's going. Did you stoke it?'

'Yes. I did it for you.' Or not exactly. In her night-time prowls she'd tossed a couple of logs on the fire at each pass. It had seemed comforting. She'd been in need of comfort, and the thought of taking the dog in there now was a good one.

'Can you get up, big boy?' Gabe asked. 'Come on, mate, let's see you live.'

Gabe was fondling him behind the ears, speaking softly, and the dog responded. He gave Gabe another of those gut wrenching looks, another moan, then heaved. He managed to stand.

Standing up, he looked like a bag of bones with a worn rug stretched over him. Only his ears were still full fur. They hinted at a dog who'd once been handsome but that time was long past.

He swayed and Gabe stooped and held him, still fondling him, while the dog leaned heavily against him.

'So you decided to come and find some help?' he said softly. 'Great decision. You're safe here. You even seem to have found a friend. Mind, you need to beware of pokers.' But he wasn't glancing up to see how she took the wisecrack; he was totally focused on the dog. 'Let's get you warm. Miss Morrissy, could you fetch us some towels, please? A lot of towels. Put some in the tumble dryer to warm them.'

'It's Nikki,' she said numbly.

'Nikki,' he repeated, but he still didn't look up.

The dog took a staggering step forward and then stopped. Enough. Gabe lifted him into his arms as if he were a featherweight, and the dog made no objection. Maybe he knew he was headed for Gabe's fireside.

Nikki headed for towels.

But, as she went, she carried the image of Gabe, a big man with his armful of dog.

He was making her heart twist.

It was the dog, she told herself fiercely. Of course it was the dog.

Only the dog. Anything else was ridiculous.

She did not need hormones.

Horse was freezing. It hadn't been raining, yet he was soaked—had he been standing in the water all night?

Nikki fetched her hairdryer. Gabe sponged the worst of the salt crust from his coat, then towelled him dry as she ran warm air over his tangled fur.

The big dog lay passive, hopeless, and Nikki felt an overwhelming urge to pick him up and hug him.

He was so big… She'd have to hug him one end at a time.

She also wanted to kill whoever had abandoned him. To do something so callous…

'Your cop friend said he was thrown from a boat.'

'He'll still feel loyal to the low-life who did it to him,' Gabe said grimly. 'I'd guess that's why he's been standing in the shallows howling.'

She sniffed. She sniffed more than once while she wielded her hairdryer, and she had to abandon her work for a bit to fetch tissues. She couldn't help herself. The emotions of the night, the emotions of the past two months, or maybe simply the emotions of now, were enough to overwhelm her. This gentle giant being betrayed in such a way…

She'd set towels by the fire for Gabe to lay him on. With her hairdryer and Gabe's toweling, they dried one side of him. Then Gabe lifted him. She replaced the sodden towels with warm ones and they dried his other side.

Gabe spoke to him all the time. Slow, gentle words of comfort. While Nikki sniffed.

Gabe's words were washing over her, reassuring her almost as much as the dog. His kindness was palpable. How could she ever have thought he'd ignore a dog in trouble on the beach? His hands stroking the dog's coat…his soft words…

He was a gruff, weathered fisherman but he cared about this dog.

He'd been rude and cold to her the day they'd met. Where was that coldness now?

She tried to imagine Jonathan doing what Gabe was doing now, and couldn't. And then she thought… what was she thinking? Comparing Gabe and Jon? Don't even think of going there.

Um…she was going there. Gabe's body was just a bit too close.

Gabe's body was making her body feel…

No. Stupid, stupid, stupid.

Focus on dog.

The big dog's body had been shuddering, great waves of cold and despair. As the warmth started to permeate, the shaking grew less. Gabe was half towelling, half stroking, all caring.

'It's okay, mate. We'll get you warm on the inside as well.'

'Do you think he got the steak?'

'I'm guessing not,' he said. 'Not in the state he's in—the food would have warmed him and he wouldn't be so hopeless. There's all sorts of predators on the beach at night—owls, rats, the odd feral cat. I'm guessing that's why he's here. He came back round the headland looking for the steak, then when we were gone he followed our scent. There was nowhere else to go.'

'Oh, Horse.'

Grown women didn't cry. Much. She concentrated fiercely on blow-drying—and realised Gabe was watching her.

'Horse?' he said.

'I've been thinking of him all night,' she said. 'In between worrying that I killed you. A dog that looks like a horse. A landlord who might have been dead.'

'Happy endings all round,' Gabe said wryly and she cast him a scared look. She knew what he was going to say. She was way in front of him.

The vet.

'Do you have any more steak?' She couldn't quite get her voice to work. She couldn't quite get her heart to work. But she wasn't going to say the vet word.

'No. You?'

'I have dinners for one. Calorie controlled.'

'Right, like Horse needs a diet.'

'I'll bring four.'

They worked on. Gabe hauled on a T-shirt and jeans and so did she, but the attention of both was on the dog. Hostilities were suspended.

The dog was so close to the edge that the sheer effort of eating seemed too much. By the look of his muzzle, he'd been sick. 'Sea water,' Gabe said grimly as he cleaned him. 'There's little fresh water round here. If he's been wandering since the van crashed he's had almost a week of nothing.'

That was a lot of speech for Gabe. They should take him to the vet, Nikki thought, but with the vet came a decision that neither of them seemed able to face. Not yet.

Save him and then decide. Dumb? Maybe, but it was what her gut was dictating, and Gabe seemed to be following the same path.

Gabe was encouraging the dog to drink, little by little. He found some sort of syringe and gently oozed water into the big dog's mouth. Once they were sure he could swallow, Nikki shredded chicken, popping tiny pieces into Horse's slack mouth and watching with satisfaction as he managed to get it down.

Slowly.

'If we feed him fast he'll be sick and we'll undo everything,' Gabe said. He sounded as if he knew what he was doing. How come he had a syringe on hand? Had he coped with injured animals before?

He was an enigma. Craggy and grim. A professional fisherman. Broad, but with muscles, there was not an inch of spare flesh on him.

He flashed from silence and anger, to caring, to tender, just like that. His hands as he cared for the big dog were gentle as could be; rough, weathered fisherman's hands fondling the dog's ears, holding the syringe, waiting with all the patience in the world for Horse to open his mouth.

Horse.

Why name a stray dog?

Why look at her landlord's hand and think…and think…?

Nothing.

She should be back on her side of the house right now, enmeshed in plans for the air conditioning system for a huge metropolitan shopping centre. The centre had been the focus of an outbreak of legionnaires' disease. Their air conditioning system needed to be revamped, and the plans needed to be finalised. Now.

Her plans were urgent—even if they bored her witless.

And Gabe should be fishing. He obviously thought that was urgent.

But nothing seemed more important than sitting by the fireside with Gabe and with Horse, gradually bringing the big dog back to life.

They were succeeding. The shuddering ceased. The dog was still limp, but he was warm and dry, and there was enough food and water going in to make them think the worst was past.

So now what?

The dog was drifting into sleep. Nikki glanced briefly at Gabe and caught a flash of pain, quickly suppressed. His head? Of course it was his head, she thought. That bruise looked horrible. What was she doing, letting him work on the dog?

'You need to sleep, too,' she told him.

'We should make a decision about this guy. Take him…'

'Let him sleep,' she said, cutting him off. 'For a bit. Then…maybe we could clean him up a bit more. If we take him back to the shelter looking lovely, then he has a better chance…'

'He's never going to look lovely,' Gabe said. 'Not even close.'

Maybe he wouldn't. The dog was carrying scars. Patches of fur had been torn away, wounds had healed but the fur hadn't grown back. An ugly scar ran the length of his left front leg. And what was he? Wolfhound? Plus the rest.

'It's drawing it out,' Gabe said and Nikki flinched. She looked down at the dog and felt ill—and then she looked at Gabe and felt her own pain reflected in his eyes.

'Not yet,' she said, suddenly fierce. 'Not until he's slept. And not until you've slept. You have the day off work. I know you're angry, and you can be as angry as you like with me, but what's done's done. Your head's hurting. Go back to bed and sleep it off, and let Horse sleep.'

'While you play Florence Nightingale to us both?'

'There's no need to be sarcastic,' she said, struggling to keep her voice even. 'A nurse is the last thing I could ever be, but it doesn't take Florence to see what you need. You and Horse both. I need to do some work…'

'You and *me* both.'

'Get over it,' she snapped. 'You're wounded, I'm not. So what I'm suggesting is that I bring my paperwork in here and do it at your dining table so I can keep an eye on Horse. I'll keep checking the fire, I'll keep offering Horse food and drink, and you go back to bed and wake up when your body lets you.'

'You'll check on me, too?'

'Every two hours,' she said firmly. 'Like a good Florence. Though I'd prefer you to leave your door open so I can make sure you're not dead all the time.'

'This is nonsense. I need to mend cray-pots.'

'You've got the day off,' she snapped. 'I told Hattie you were ill. Don't make a liar of me.'

'You really will look after the dog?'

'I'll look after both of you, until you wake up. Then…' She glanced down at Horse and looked away. 'Then we'll do what comes next.'

He rang Raff from the privacy of his bedroom. The Banksia Bay cop answered on the first ring. 'Why aren't you at sea?' Raff demanded. 'Hattie says you hit your head. I thought you sounded bad last night. You want some help?'

This town, Gabe thought grimly. Banksia Bay was a great place to live unless you hankered for privacy. He did hanker for privacy, but he loved the place and intrusion was the price he paid.

'And Hattie says your tenant's looking after you.

Mate…' Raff drew the word out—*maaate*. It was a question all by itself.

'She hit me,' he said before he could help himself.

'Did she now.' Raff thought about that for a bit. 'She had her reasons?'

Nip that one in the bud. 'She thought I was a bunyip. She was searching for the dog. I was searching for the dog. We collided. She was carrying a poker. And that goes no further than you,' he said sharply, as he heard a choke of laughter on the end of the line.

'Scout's honour,' Raff said.

'We never made Scouts.' Raff had been one of the town's bad boys. Like him.

'That's what I mean. You need any help?'

'No. We found the dog. That's why I'm ringing.'

'*We* found the dog? You and Miss Morrissy?'

'Nikki,' he said before he could help himself and he heard the interest sharpen.

'Curiouser and curiouser. So you and Nikki…'

'The dog's here,' he snapped. 'Fed and watered and asleep by my fire. I'll bring him down to Fred when I've had a sleep.'

'You're having a sleep?'

'Nikki's orders,' he said and suddenly he had an urge to smile. Quickly suppressed. 'She's bossy.'

'Well, well.'

'And you can just put that right out of your head,' he snapped. 'I don't want a dog, and I don't want a woman even more. Tell Henrietta the dog's found and we'll take him to Fred tonight.'

'We?'

'Go find some villains to chase,' he growled. 'My head hurts. I'm going to sleep.'

'On Nikki's orders?'

He told Raff where to put his interest, and he hung up. Stripped to his boxers again. Climbed into bed. Following orders.

His head really did hurt.

She was going to check on him every two hours. The thought was…

Nope. He didn't know what the thought was.

He didn't want her checking him every two hours. *'I'd prefer you to leave your door open so I can make sure you're not dead…'*

He sighed and opened his door. Glanced across at Nikki, who glanced back. Waved. He glowered and dived under the covers.

He didn't want a woman in his living room.

Nor did he want a dog.

What was he doing, in bed in the middle of the morning?

He put his head on the pillow and the aching eased. Maybe she had a point. A man had to be sensible.

He fell asleep thinking of the dog.

Trying not to think of Nikki.

* * *

It was so domestic it was almost claustrophobic. The fire, the dog, Gabe asleep right through the door.

The work she was doing was tidying up plans she'd already drawn—nothing complex, which was just as well the way she was feeling. Her head was all over the place.

Biggest thought? Gabe.

No. Um, no, it wasn't. Or it shouldn't be. Her biggest thought had to be—could she keep a dog?

As a kid she'd thought she might like a dog. That was never going to happen, though. Her parents were high-flyers, both lawyers with an international clientele. They loved her to bits in the time they could spare for her, but that time was limited. She was an only child, taken from country to country, from boarding school to international hotel to luxury resort.

And after childhood? University, followed by a top paying job, a gorgeous apartment. Then Jonathan.

Maybe she could get a small white fluff ball, she'd thought occasionally, when she was missing Jon. When he was supposedly working elsewhere. But where would a dog fit into a lifestyle similar to her parents'?

And now...

Her job still took her away.

Her job didn't have to take her away. Or not for long. She could glean enough information from a

site visit to keep her working for months. Most que-
ries could be sorted online—there was never a lot
of use stomping round construction sites.

She quite liked stomping round construction sites.
It was the part of her job she enjoyed most.

It was the only part…

Salary? Prestige?

Both were less and less satisfying. Her parents
thought her career was wonderful. Jonathan thought
it was wonderful. But now…

Now was hardly the time to be thinking of a career change. She was good at what she did. She was
paid almost embarrassingly well. She could afford
to pay others to do the menial stuff.

So maybe a little white fluff ball?

Or Horse.

Horse was hardly a fluff ball. Ten times as big,
and a lot more needy.

Maybe she could share parenting with Gabe, she
thought. When she was needed on site, he could stay
home from sea.

Shared parenting? Of a dog who looked like a
mangy horse, with a grumpy landlord fisherman?

With a body to die for. And with the gentlest of
hands. And a voice that said he cared.

She glanced across the passage. The deal was she
wouldn't check on him every two hours as long as
he kept his door open.

If he dropped dead, she was on the wrong side of the passage.

There wasn't a lot she could do if he dropped dead.

At least the dog was breathing. She watched his chest rise and fall, rise and fall. He was flopped as close to the fire as he could be without being burned. Gabe had set the screen so no ember could fly out, but she suspected he wouldn't wake even if it did.

He looked like a dog used to being hurt.

Maybe he'd be vicious when he recovered.

Maybe her landlord wouldn't let her keep a dog.

Was she really thinking about keeping him?

It was just…

The last few weeks had been desolate. It was all very well saying she wanted a sea change, but there wasn't enough work to fill the day and the night, and the nights were long and silent. She'd left Sydney in rage and in grief, and at night it came back to haunt her.

She also found the nights, the country noises… creepy.

'Because of guys like you howling on beaches,' she said out loud, and Horse raised his head and looked at her. Then sighed and set his head down again, as if it was too heavy to hold up.

How could someone throw him off a boat?

A great wounded mutt.

Her new best friend?

She glanced across the passage again. Gabe was deeply asleep, his bedding barely covering his hips.

He was wounded too, she thought, and with a flash of insight she thought it wasn't just the hit over the head with the poker. He was living in a house built for a dozen, a mile out of town, on his own. Not even a dog.

'He needs a dog, too,' she told Horse.

Shared parenting was an excellent solution.

'Yes, but that's complicated.' She set down her pen and crossed to Gabe's bedroom door to make sure his chest was rising and falling. It was, but the sight of his chest did things to her own chest…

There went those hormones again. She had to figure a way of reining them in.

Return to dog. Immediately.

She knelt and fondled the big dog's ears. He stirred and moaned, a long, low doggy moan containing all the pathos in the world.

She put her head down close to his. Almost nose to nose. 'It's okay,' she said. 'I've given up on White and Fluffy. And I think I do like dogs. You're not going to the vet.'

A great shaggy paw came up and touched her shoulder.

Absurdly moved, she found herself hugging him. Her arms were full of dog. His great brown eyes were enormous.

Could she keep him?

'My parents would have kittens,' she told him.

Her mother was in Helsinki doing something important.

Her father was in New York.

'Yes, and I'm here,' she told Horse, giving in to the weirdly comforting sensation of holding a dog close, feeling the warmth of him. 'I'm here by the fire with you, and our landlord's just over the passage. He's grumpy, but underneath I reckon he's a pussycat. I reckon he might let you stay.'

The fire was magnificently warm. She hadn't had enough sleep last night.

She hesitated and then hauled some cushions down from the settee. She settled beside Horse. He sighed, but it was a different sigh. As if things might be looking up.

'Perfect,' said Nikkita Morrissy, specialist air conditioning engineer, sea-changer, tenant. She snuggled on the cushions and Horse stirred a bit and heaved himself a couple of inches so she was closer. 'Let's settle in for the long haul. You and me— and Gabe if he wants to join us. If my hit on the head hasn't killed him. Welcome to our new life.'

CHAPTER FOUR

GABE woke and it was still daylight. It took time to figure exactly why he was in bed, why the clock was telling him it was two in the afternoon, and why a woman and a dog were curled up on cushions on his living room floor.

Horse.

Nikki.

Nikki was asleep beside Horse?

The dog didn't fit with the image of the woman. Actually, nothing fitted. He was having trouble getting his thoughts in order.

He should be a hundred miles offshore. Every day the boat was in harbour cost money.

Um…he had enough money. He needed to forget fishing, at least for a day.

He was incredibly, lazily comfortable. How long since he'd lain in bed and just…lain? Not slept, just stared at the ceiling, thought how great the sheets felt on his naked skin, how great it was that the warm sea breeze wafted straight in through his bedroom window and made him feel that the sea was right here.

Lots of fishermen—lots of his crew—took themselves as far from the sea as possible when they weren't working. Not Gabe. The sea was a part of him.

He'd always been a loner. As a kid, the beach was an escape from the unhappiness in the house. His parents' marriage was bitter and often violent. His father was passionately possessive of his much younger wife, sharing her with no one. If Gabe spent time with his mother, his father reacted with a resentment that Gabe soon learned to fear. His survival technique was loneliness.

As he got older, the boat became his escape as well.

And then there was his brief marriage. Yeah, well, that had taught him the sea was his only real constant. People hurt. Solitude was the only way to go.

Even dogs broke your heart.

Sixteen years…

'Get another one fast.' Fred, the Banksia Bay vet, had been brusque. 'The measure of a life well lived is how many good dogs you can fit into it. I'm seventy years old and I'm up to sixteen and counting. It's torn a hole in my gut every time I've lost one, and the only way I can fill it is finding another. And you know what? Every single one of them stays with me. They're all part of who I am. The gut gets bigger.' He'd patted his ample stomach. 'Get another.'

Or not. Did Fred know just how big a hole Jem had left?

Don't think about it.

Watch Nikki instead.

He lay and watched woman and dog sleeping, just across the passage. Strangers seldom entered his house. Not even friends. And no one slept by his fire but him.

Until now.

She looked...okay.

She'd wake soon, and she'd be gone. This moment would be past, but for now... For now it felt strangely okay that she was here. For now he let the comfort of her presence slide into his bones, easing parts of him he didn't know were hurting. A dog and a woman asleep before his fire...

He closed his eyes and sleep reclaimed him.

She woke and it was three o'clock and Horse was squatting on his haunches rather than sprawled on his side. His head was cocked to one side, as if he was trying to figure her out. Sitting up! That had to be good.

She hugged him. She fed him. He ate a little, drank a little. She opened the French windows and asked him if he needed to go outside but he politely declined, by putting his head back on his paws and dozing again.

She thought about going back to work.

The plans on the table were supremely uninteresting. Engineering had sounded cool when she enrolled at university. Doing stuff.

Not sitting drawing endless plans of endless air conditioning systems, no matter how complex.

Gabe's living room, however, was lined with bookshelves, and the bookshelves were crammed with books.

And photograph albums. Her secret vice.

Other people's families.

Nikki had been sent to boarding school at seven. If friends invited her home for the holidays her parents were relieved, so she'd spent much of her childhood looking at families from the outside in.

Brothers, sisters, grandmas, uncles and aunts. You didn't get a lot of those the way she was raised.

Her friends could never understand her love of photograph albums, but she hadn't grown out of it, and here were half a dozen, right within reach.

A girl had to read something. Or draw plans.

No choice.

The first four albums were those of a child, an adolescent, a young woman. School friends, beach, hiking, normal stuff. Nikki had albums like this herself, photographs taken with her first camera.

The albums must belong to Gabe's mother, she

decided. The girl and then the woman looked a bit like Gabe. She was much smaller, compact, neat. But she looked nice. She had the same dark hair as Gabe, the same thoughtful eyes. She saw freckles and a shy smile in the girl, and then the woman.

After school, her albums differed markedly from Nikki's. This woman hadn't spent her adolescence at university. The first post-school pictures were of her beside stone walls, wearing dungarees, heavy boots, thick gloves. The smile became cheeky, a woman gaining confidence.

There were photos of stone walls.

Lots of stone walls.

Nikki glanced outside to the property boundary, where a stone wall ran along the road, partly built, as if it had stopped mid-construction. Wires ran along the unfinished part to make it a serviceable fence.

She turned back to the next album. Saw the beginnings of romance. A man, considerably older than the girl, thickset, a bit like Gabe as well, looking as if he was struggling to find a smile for the camera. Holding the girl possessively.

An album of a wedding. Then a baby.

Gabe.

Really cute, she thought, and glanced across the passage and thought…you really could see the man in the baby.

Gabe before life had weathered him.

The photos were all of Gabe now—Gabe until he was about seven, sturdy, cheeky, laughing.

Then nothing. The final album had five pages of pictures and the rest lay empty.

What had happened? Divorce? Surely a young mum would keep on taking pictures. Surely she'd take these albums with her.

She set the albums back in place, and her attention was caught by a set of books just above. *The Art of Stone Walling. The Stone Walls of Yorkshire.* More.

She flicked through, fascinated, caught in intricacies of stone walling.

Gabe slept on.

She was learning how to build stone walls. In theory.

She'd kind of like to try.

She reached the end of the first book as Horse struggled to his feet and crossed to the French windows. Pawed.

Bathroom.

But… Escape?

Visions of Horse standing up to his haunches in the shallows sprang to mind. She daren't risk letting him go. The faded curtains were looped back with tasseled cords, perfect for fashioning a lead.

'Okay, let's go but don't pull,' she told him. At full strength this dog could tow two of her, but he was wobbly.

She cast a backward glance at Gabe. Still sleeping. Quick check. Chest rising and falling.

She and Horse were free to do as they pleased.

When Gabe woke again the sun was sinking low behind Black Mountain. He'd slept the whole day?

His head felt great. He felt great all over. He was relaxed and warm and filled with a sense of well-being he hadn't felt since…who knew?

He rolled lazily onto his side and gazed out of the window.

And froze.

For a moment he thought he was dreaming. There was a woman in the garden, her back to him, crouched over a pile of stones. Sorting.

A dog lay by her side, big and shaggy.

Nikki and Horse.

Nikki held up a stone, inspected it, said something to Horse, then shifted so she could place it into the unfinished stretch of stone wall.

He felt as if the oxygen was being sucked from the room.

A memory blasting back…

His mother, crouched over the stones, the wall so close to finished. Thin, drawn, exhausted. Setting down her last stone. Weeping. Hugging him.

'I can't…'

'Mum, what's wrong?'

'I'm so tired. Gabe, very soon I'll need to go to

sleep.' But using a voice that said this wasn't a normal sleep she was talking about.

Then…desolation.

His father afterwards, kicking stones, kicking everything. His mother's old dog, yelping, running for the cover Gabe could never find.

'Dad, could we finish the wall?' It had taken a month to find the courage to ask.

'It's finished.' A sharp blow across his head. 'Don't you understand, boy, it's finished.'

He understood it now. Nikki had to understand it, too.

People hurt. You didn't try and interfere. Unless there was trouble you let people be and they let you be. You didn't try and change things.

He should have put it in the tenancy agreement.

Stone wall building was weirdly satisfying on all sorts of levels.

She'd always loved puzzles, as she'd loved building things. To transform a pile of stones into a wall as magnificent as this…

Wide stones had been set into the earth to form the base, then irregular stones piled higher and higher, two outer levels with small stones between. Wider stones were layed crosswise over both sides every foot or so, binding both sides together. No stone was the same. Each position was carefully assessed, each stone considered from all angles. Tried. Tried again. As she was doing now.

She'd set eight stones in an hour and was feeling as if she'd achieved something amazing.

This could be a whole new hobby, she thought. She could finish the wall.

Horse lay by her side, dozy but watchful, warm in the afternoon sunshine. Every now and then he cast a doubtful glance towards the beach but she'd fashioned a tie from the curtain cords, she had him tethered and she talked to him as she worked.

'I know. You loved him but he rejected you. You and me both. Jonathan and your scum-bag owner. Broken hearts club, that's us. We need a plan to get over it. I'm not sure what our plan should be, but while we're waiting for something to occur this isn't bad.' She held up a stone. 'You think this'll fit?'

The dog cocked his head; seemed to consider.

The pain that had clenched in her chest for months eased a little. Unknotted in the sharing, and in the work.

She would have liked to be a builder.

She thought suddenly of a long ago careers exhibition. At sixteen she'd been unsure of what she wanted to do. She'd gone to the career exhibition with school and almost the first display was a carpenter, working on a delicate coffee table. While other students moved from one display to the next, she stopped, entranced.

After half an hour he'd invited her to help, and she'd stayed with him until her teachers came to find her.

'I'll need to get an apprenticeship to be a carpenter,' she'd told her father the next time she'd seen him, breathless with certainty that she'd found her calling.

But her father was due to catch the dawn flight to New York. He'd scheduled two hours' quality time with his daughter and he didn't intend wasting it on nonsense.

'Of course society needs builders, but for you, my girl, with your brains, the sky's the limit. We'll get you into Law—Oxford? Cambridge?'

Even her chosen engineering degree had met with combined parental disapproval, even though it was specialist engineering leading to a massive salary. But here, now... She remembered that long ago urge to build things, to create.

Air conditioning systems didn't compare. Endless plans.

Another stone...This was so difficult. It had to be perfect.

'What do you think you're doing?'

She managed to suppress a yelp, but only just. Gabe was dressed again, in jeans and T-shirt. He'd come up behind her. His face was like thunder, his voice was dripping ice.

He was blocking her sun. Even Horse backed and whimpered.

The sheer power of the man…the anger…

It was as much as she could do not to back and run.

Not her style, she thought grimly. This man had her totally disconcerted but whimpering was never an option. 'I thought I'd try and do some…' she faltered.

'Don't.'

'Don't you want it finished? I thought…I've been reading the books from your living room.'

'You've been reading my mother's books?'

Uh-oh. She'd desecrated a shrine?

'I'm sorry. I…'

'You had no right.'

'No.' She lifted the book she'd been referring to. Caught her breath. Decided she'd hardly committed murder. 'I'll put this back,' she said placatingly. 'No damage done. I don't think I've done anything appalling.'

But then…he'd scared her. Again.

Shock was turning to indignation.

He was angry?

She met his gaze full on. Tilted her chin.

Horse nosed her ankle. She let her hand drop to his rough coat and the feel of him was absurdly comforting.

What was with this guy? Why did he make her

feel—how he made her feel? She couldn't describe it. She only knew that she was totally confused.

'I've only fitted eight stones,' she said, forcing her tone down a notch. Even attempting a smile. 'You want me to take them out again?'

'Leave it.' His voice was still rough, but the edges of anger were blunted. He took the book from her. Glanced at it. Glanced away. 'How's the dog?'

'He's fine.' She was still indignant. He sounded... cold.

The normal Gabe?

A man she should back away from.

'We need to make a decision,' he said.

'I have,' she said and tilted her chin still further. 'Hi!'

The new voice made them both swivel. A woman was at the gate. She was middle-aged and sensibly dressed, in moleskin trousers and a battered fleecy jacket. She swung the gate open and Horse whined and backed away.

Even from twenty yards away Nikki saw the woman flinch.

'It's okay,' the woman said, gentling her voice as she approached. 'I hate it that I lock these guys up and they react accordingly. I can't help that I'm associated with their life's low point.'

Horse whined again. Nikki felt him tug against the cord. She wasn't all that sure of it holding.

Gabe was suddenly helping. His hand was on the

big dog's neck, helping her hold on to her curtain-fashioned collar. Touching hers. His hand was large and firm—and once more caring?

Where had that thought come from? But she felt Horse relax and she knew the dog felt the same. Even if this guy did get inexplicably angry, there was something at his core...

'Raff told me you'd found him,' the woman was saying. 'Hi, Gabe.' She came forward, her hand extended to Nikki, a blunt gesture of greeting. 'We haven't met. I'm Henrietta. I run the local dog shelter. This guy's one of mine.'

Horse whimpered and tried to go behind Nikki's legs. Nikki's hand tightened on his collar—and so did Gabe's.

Hands touching. Warmth. Strength. Nikki didn't pull away, even though Henrietta's hand was still extended, even though she knew Gabe could hold him.

'You want me to take him?' Henrietta asked.

No.

Her decision had already been made but she needed Gabe's consent. He was, after all, her landlord.

'I'd like to keep him,' she said, more loudly than she intended, and there was a moment's silence.

Henrietta's grim expression relaxed, then did more than relax. It curved into a wide grin that practically spilt her face. But then she caught herself, her smile was firmly repressed and her expression became businesslike.

'Are you in a position to offer him a good home?'

'Am I?' she asked Gabe. 'I think I am,' she said diffidently. 'But Gabe's my landlord. I'll need his permission.'

'You're asking me to keep him?' Gabe's demand was incredulous.

'No,' she said flatly. Some time during this afternoon her world had shifted. She wasn't exactly sure where it had shifted; she only knew that things were changing and Horse was an important part of that change. 'I want to keep him myself. Just me.' Her life was her own, she thought, suddenly resolute. No men need apply.

No man—not even her landlord—was needed to share her dog.

'I need to do a bit of reorganisation,' she said, speaking now to Henrietta. 'At the moment I'm working away...'

'I can't look after him,' Gabe said bluntly. 'Not when I'm at sea.'

'I'm not asking you to,' she flashed back at him. There were things going on with Gabe she didn't understand. He had her disconcerted, but for now she needed to focus only on Horse. And her future. Gabe had to be put third.

'I'm reorganising my career,' she told Henrietta. 'At the end of this month and maybe next, I'll need to go away for a few days. After that I won't need to.' That was simple enough. She'd hand her international clients over to her colleagues.

Her colleagues would think she was nuts.

Her colleagues as in Jonathan?

Don't go there.

Could she keep working for him?

'I might even be rethinking my career altogether,' she said, a bit more brusquely than she intended. She glanced down at the stones and then glanced away again, astounded where her thoughts were taking her. How absurd to think she could ever do something so…so wonderful.

Was she crazy? This surely could only ever be a hobby.

Concentrate on Horse. The rest was nonsense. Fanciful thinking after an upset night. 'Whatever I do, I've decided I can keep Horse,' she managed. 'If I can get some help for the first two months.'

But Gabe was looking at her as if she was something that had just crawled out of the cheese.

'You've decided this all since last night?' he demanded. 'Do you know how much of a commitment a dog is? He's not a handbag, picked up and discarded on a whim. Sixteen years…'

'We're not talking Jem here,' Henrietta said sharply.

'Jem?'

'Gabe's dog,' Henrietta told her. 'Gabe found

Jem on the beach sixteen years ago. She died three months back.'

'I'm sorry,' Nikki said, disconcerted, but her apologies weren't required or wanted. Gabe's face was rigid with anger.

'We're not talking Jem. We're talking you. What do you know about dogs?'

'I'll learn.'

'You mean you know nothing.'

'You're trying to talk me out of keeping him?'

'I'm talking sense.'

'I can keep him for the days you're away,' Henrietta interjected, but she was watching Gabe. 'I run a boarding kennel alongside the shelter, so if you really are going to reorganise…'

'You'd let her keep him?' Gabe's voice was incredulous.

'It's that or put him down,' Henrietta snapped. 'Nikki's offering.'

'And if I say no?'

There was a general intake of breath. If he said no…

What would she do?

Take Horse and live elsewhere? Somewhere that wasn't here? There were so few rental options.

Go back to Sydney.

No! Here was scary, but Sydney was scarier.

Move on. Who knew where? With dog?

This was dumb. To move towns because of a dog…

But this afternoon she'd felt his heartbeat as he slept. The thought of ending that heartbeat…

Horse was as lost as she was, she thought, and she glanced at Gabe and thought there were three of them. She could see pain behind Gabe's anger; behind his blank refusal to help.

She couldn't think of Gabe's pain now. She'd do this alone.

No. She'd do it with Horse.

'He's my dog,' she said, making her voice firm.

Henrietta turned to Gabe. 'So. Let's get this straight. Are you planning on evicting Nikki because she has a dog?'

'She doesn't know what she's letting herself in for.'

'You work at home, right?' Henrietta asked her, obviously deciding to abandon Gabe's arguments as superfluous.

'Yes.'

'Fantastic. When do you need to go away again?'

She did a frantic mental reshuffle. 'I can put it off for a while. Three weeks…'

'Then you have three weeks to learn all about dogs,' Henrietta decreed. 'If at the end of that time you decide you can't keep him then we'll rethink things. So Gabe… I have a happy ending in view. What about you? You'll seriously evict her if she keeps him?'

They were all looking at him. Nikki and Henrietta…Even Horse seemed to understand his future hung on what Gabe said right now.

'Fine,' he said explosively.

'That's not what I want to hear,' Henrietta said. 'How about a bit of enthusiasm?'

'You expect me to be enthusiastic that there's a dog about to live here? With a totally untrained owner?'

'You're trained,' Henrietta said. 'I'd feel happier if you were offering, but I have a feeling this guy will settle for what he can get. If the heart's in the right place, the rest can follow, eh, Nikki?'

'I…yes,' she said weakly, wondering where exactly her heart was.

'That's great,' Henrietta said and patted Horse. who was still looking nervous. 'What will you call him?'

'Horse,' Nikki said. 'I'll need stuff. I don't know what. Can you tell me?'

'Gabe might give you a…' Henrietta started and then glanced again at Gabe. Winced. 'Okay, maybe not. Let's take your new dog inside and I'll make you a list myself. Unless you want to evict her first, Gabe?'

'I'm going to the boat,' he snapped. 'Be it on your head.'

He headed for the boat, away from women, away from dog. Away from stuff he didn't want to deal with.

He needed to sort cray-pots, mend some. He

started but it didn't keep his head from wandering. He kept seeing Nikki, sorting through her pile of rocks. *His mother's pile of rocks.*

He kept seeing Nikki curled in front of the fire, sleeping beside Horse.

Horse. It was a stupid name for a dog.

What was also stupid was his reaction, he told himself. What was the big deal? His tenant had found herself a dog. It was nothing to do with him. As for the stone walling...

She wouldn't touch it again.

Why not let her finish it?

Stupid or not, he felt as if he was right on the edge of a whirlpool, and he was being pulled inexorably inside.

He'd been there before.

There was nothing inside but pain.

The cray-pots weren't hard enough.

He'd check the *Lady Nell*'s propeller, he decided. It had fouled last time out. They'd got it clear but maybe it'd be wise to give it a thorough check.

Ten minutes later he had a scuba tank on, lowering himself over the side.

He should do this with someone on board keeping watch. If there was an accident...

If there was an accident no one gave a toss; it was his business what he did with his life.

He had scores of employees, dependent on him for their livelihood.

He also had one tenant. Dependent?

If Horse decided to head for the beach again, he was bigger than she could possibly hold.

It was none of his business. She didn't need him. The dog didn't need him. No one did. Even if something happened to him, the legal stuff was set up so this town's fishing fleet would survive.

How morbid was that? He was about to check a propeller. He'd done it a hundred times.

He needed to see things in perspective.

He dived underwater. Right now underwater seemed safer than the surface—and a whole lot clearer.

Henrietta left and came back with supplies, and Nikki was set. Dog food, dog bed, dog bowls. Collar, lead, treats, ball times six... Practically a car full.

'You'll need a kennel, but they don't come prefabricated in Horse's size,' Henrietta told her. 'I've brought you a trampoline bed instead. You'll need to get a kennel built by winter. Oh, and there's no need to spread it round town that I've brought this. Normally my new owners need to show me their preparations before I'll agree to let them have the dog.'

'So why the special treatment?' Nikki had made tea. Henrietta was sipping Earl Grey from one of Nikki's dainty cups, looking a bit uncomfortable. Maybe she ought to buy some mugs.

Maybe her life was going to change in a few other ways, she thought. Her apartment was furnished with the elegant possessions she'd acquired for the Sydney apartment. Some her parents had given her. Some she and Jon had chosen together. This teaset was antique, given to her by Jon for her last birthday.

The owner of a dog like Horse wouldn't serve tea in cups like this. She hadn't thought it through until now, but maybe she should shop…

'I hate putting dogs down,' Henrietta was saying. 'Sometimes, though, I don't have a choice. I can't keep them all. And if potential owners don't care enough to commit to buying or scrounging dog gear, then they don't care enough to be entrusted to a dog. These dogs have been through enough. I'd rather put them down than sentence them to more misery.'

'But me…'

'You live with Gabe,' Henrietta said simply. 'You mistreat Horse, you'll have him to answer to. Even if he says it's nothing to do with him, he'll be watching. And that's the second thing. This place without a dog is wrong. Gabe needs a dog. If he gets it via you, that's fine by me.'

'He's not getting him via me. This is my call. My dog.'

'Yes, but you live with Gabe,' Henrietta repeated, and finished her tea in one noisy gulp. 'Living so close, you're almost family, and now you have a dog. Welcome to Banksia Bay, and welcome to your new role as dog owner. Any more questions, ask Gabe. He's grumpy and dour and always a loner but he has reason to be. Underneath he's a good man, and he'll never let a dog suffer. He treated Jem like gold.' Then she hesitated. Made to say something. Hesitated again.

Nikki watched her face. Wondered what she'd been about to say. Then asked what she'd like to know. 'Could you tell me about him?' she ventured. 'What happened to his mother?'

Henrietta considered for a long moment and then shrugged.

'I shouldn't say, but why not? If you don't hear it from me you'll hear it from a hundred other people in this town. Okay, potted history. Gabe's mother died of cancer when he was eight. His dad was an oaf and a bully. He was also a miser. He forced Gabe to leave school at fourteen, used him as an unpaid deck hand. Maybe Gabe would have left but luckily—and I will say luckily—he died when Gabe was eighteen. He left a fortune. He left no will, so Gabe inherited. Gabe was a kid, floundering, desperately unhappy—and suddenly rich. So along came Lisbette, a selfish cow, all surface glitter, taking advantage of little more than a boy. She married him and she fleeced him, just like that.'

'Oh, no…'

'I'd have horsewhipped her if I'd had my way,' Henrietta said grimly. 'But she was gone. And Gabe took it hard. He still had his dad's boat and this house, but little else. So he took Jem and headed off to the West, to the oil rigs. A good seaman can make a lot if he's prepared to take risks and, from what I can gather, Gabe took more than a few. Then the fishing here started to falter and suddenly Gabe returned. He's good with figures, good with fishing, good with people. He almost single-handedly pulled the fleet back together. But he's shut himself off for years and so far the only one to touch that is Jem.' She touched the big dog's soft ears. 'So maybe… maybe this guy can do the same. Or maybe even his owner can.'

'Sorry?' Nikki said, startled.

'Just thinking,' Henrietta said hastily, and rose to leave. 'Dreaming families for my dogs is what I do. Good luck to the three of you.'

She looked at the teacup. Grinned. 'Amazing,' she said. 'They say owners end up looking like their dogs. These cups fit poodles, not wolfhounds.' She grinned down at Horse, asleep draped over Nikki's feet, and then looked back to Nikki. 'Poodle,' she said. 'Maybe now, but not for much longer. I'm looking forward to big changes around here. For everyone.'

* * *

Gabe slipped underwater, checked the propeller and inspected the hull. Minutely. It was the best checked hull in the fleet. Then he went back to mending cray-pots. By nine he was the only person in the harbour.

The rest of his boats were out, and he was stuck on dry land. Because of Nikki.

What was she about, removing his alarm? Telling Hattie to go without him?

He'd needed to sleep, he conceded. His head still ached.

Because she'd hit him.

It was an accident. She meant no harm.

She meant to keep the dog. Horse.

It was a stupid name for a dog. A dog needed a bit of dignity.

Dignity.

She'd have to get that fur unmatted, he thought, and getting the tangles out of that neglected coat was a huge job. Did she know what she was letting herself in for?

It was nothing to do with him. Nothing! He wasn't going near.

She was living right next door to him. With her dog who needed detangling.

He'd yelled at her. Because she'd picked up a few rocks.

He'd behaved appallingly.

Why?

He knew why. And it wasn't the memory of his mother. It wasn't the dog. It was more.

It couldn't be more. He didn't want more, and more wasn't going to happen.

It was dark. Time to head home.

Maybe he could take Jem's old brushes across to her. A peace offering.

That wasn't more. It was sensible. It felt…okay.

But when he got home there wasn't a light on, apart from the security light he kept on in the shared porch.

Were she and the dog asleep?

She'd slept this afternoon. He'd seen her, curled on the hearth with the dog.

With Horse.

They were nothing to do with him.

He glanced at the gap in the stone wall. Sensed the faint echo of Nikki. And Horse.

By his side… Shades of Jem.

He was going nuts. The hit on his head had obviously been harder than he thought. Ghosts were everywhere, even to the feel of Jem beside him. Jem had always been with him, on the boat, under his bed, by the fire, a heartbeat by his side.

Whoa, he was maudlin. Get over it.

Disoriented, he found himself heading for the

beach. A man could stare at the sea in the moon-light. Find some answers?

But the only answers he found on the beach were Nikki and Horse.

CHAPTER FIVE

THEY were sitting just above the high water mark, right near the spot where Horse had stood and howled last night. Gabe saw them straight away, unmistakable, the silhouette of the slight woman and the huge, rangy dog framed against a rising moon.

Maybe he'd better call out. Warn her of his approach. Who knew what she was carrying tonight?

'Nikki!'

She turned. So did Horse, uttering a low threatening growl that suddenly turned into an unsure whine. Maybe the dog was as confused as he was.

'Gabe?' She couldn't see him—he was still in shadows. She sounded scared.

'It's Gabe.' He said it quickly, before she fired the poker.

'Are you still angry?'

Deep breath. Get this sorted. Stop being an oaf. 'I need to apologise,' he said, walking across the beach to them. 'I was out of line. Whether you keep Horse is none of my business. And snapping about the stones was nuts. Can we blame it on the hit on the head and move on?'

'Sure,' she said, but she sounded wary. 'I did hit you. I guess I can afford to cut you some slack.'

'Thank you,' he said gravely. 'Are you two moon watching?'

'Horse refuses to settle.' She shifted along the log she was perched on so there was room for him as well. 'He whined and whined, so finally I figured we might as well come down here and see that no one's coming. So he can finally settle into our new life.'

'Your new life?' he said cautiously, sorting wheat from chaff. 'You really intend changing your life?'

'My life is changed anyway,' she said. 'That's what comes of falling for a king-sized rat. It's messed with my serenity no end.'

Don't ask. It was none of his business.

But she wasn't expecting him to ask. She was staring out to sea, talking almost to herself, and her self containment touched him as neediness never could.

Since when had he ever wanted to be involved?

Horse nuzzled his hand. He patted the dog and said, 'You fell for a king-sized rat?'

Had he intended to ask? Surely not.

'My boss.'

He had no choice now.

'You want to tell me about it?'

* * *

She had no intention of telling him. She hadn't told anyone. The guy she'd thought she loved was married.

Her parents knew she'd split with Jonathan but both her parents were on their third or fourth partner; splits were no big deal. And in the office, to her friends, she'd hung onto her pride. Her pride seemed like all she had left.

But here, now, sitting on the beach with Horse between them, pride and privacy no longer seemed important.

So she told him. Bluntly. Dispassionately, as if it had happened to someone else, not to her.

'Jonathan Ostler of Ostler Engineering,' she said, her voice cool and hard. 'International engineering designer. Smooth, rich, efficient. Hates mixing business with pleasure. My boss. He asked me out four years ago. Six months later we were sharing an apartment but no one in the office was to know. Jonathan thought it'd mess with company morale. So... In the office we were so businesslike you wouldn't believe. If we were coming to work at the same time we'd split up a block away so we'd never arrive together. He addressed me as Nikki but I addressed him as Mr Ostler. Strictly formal.'

'Sounds weird.'

'Yes, but I could see his point,' she said. 'Sleeping with the boss is hardly the way to endear yourself to the rest of the staff, and Jon was overseas so much it wasn't an effort. A few people knew we were together but not many. So there I was, dream job, dream guy, dream apartment, four years. Dreaming weddings, if you must know. Starting to be anxious he didn't want to settle, but too stupidly in love to push it. Then two months ago there was an explosion in a factory where we'd been overseeing changes. The call came in the middle of the night—hysterical—our firm could be sued for millions. Jon caught the dawn plane to Düsseldorf with minutes to spare, and in the rush he left his mobile phone sitting on his—on *our*—bedside table. The next day our office was crazy. The Düsseldorf situation was frightening and the phone was going nuts. Jonathan's phone. Finally, I answered it. It was Jonathan's wife. In London. Their eight-year-old had been in a car accident. Please could I tell her where Jon was.'

'Ouch.'

'I coped,' she said, a tinge of pride warming her voice as she remembered that ghastly moment. 'I made sympathetic noises. I made sure Jonathan Junior wasn't in mortal danger, I got the details. Then I left a message with the manager of the Düsseldorf factory, asking Jon to phone his wife. I told him to say the message was from Nikki. Then I moved out of our apartment. Jonathan returned a week later, and I'd already arranged to move here, to do my work via the Internet.'

'But you still work for him?'

'Personal and business don't mix.'

'Like hell they don't,' he snapped. 'I've had relationships go sour between the crew. It messes with staff morale no end, and there's no way they can work together afterwards.'

'I'm good at my work.' But her uncertainty was growing and she couldn't put passion into her voice. 'The pay's great.'

'Can you work for yourself?'

'It's a specialist industry,' she said. 'I couldn't set up in competition to Jon. I could work for someone else, but it would have to be overseas.'

'So why not go overseas?'

'I don't want to.' But she'd been thinking. Thinking and thinking. She'd been totally, hopelessly in love with Jonathan for years and to change her life so dramatically...

Why not change it more?

Tomorrow. Think of it tomorrow.

'And now I have a dog,' she said, hauling herself back to the here and now with something akin to desperation. 'So here I am.' Deep breath. Tomorrow? Why not say now? 'But I have been thinking of changing jobs. Changing completely.'

'To what?'

How to say it? It was ridiculous. And to say stone walling, when she knew how he felt...

But the germ of an idea that had started today wouldn't go away.

Putting one stone after another into a wall.

Crazy. To turn her back on specialist training…

Oh, but how satisfying.

It was a whim, she reminded herself sharply. A whim of today. Tomorrow it'd be gone and she'd be back to sensible.

Don't talk about it. Don't push this man further than you already have.

'I don't know,' she managed. 'All I know is that I need something. Woman needs change.' She hugged Horse, who was still gazing out to sea. 'Woman needs dog.'

'No one needs a dog.'

'Says you who just lost one. I wonder if Horse's owner misses him like you miss Jem.'

'Nikki…'

'Don't stick my nose into what's not my business? You've been telling me that all day. But now… I've told you about my non existent love life. You want to tell me why I can't finish your stone wall?'

'It's my mother's wall.'

'And she disapproves of completion?'

'She died when I was a child. She didn't get to finish it.'

'So the hole's like a shrine,' she said cautiously, like one might approach an unexploded grenade. 'I can see that. But you know, if it was me I'd want the wall finished. Are you sure your mum's not up there fretting? You know, I'm a neat freak. If I die

with my floor half-hoovered, feel welcome to finish it. In fact I'll haunt you if you don't.'

'You don't like an unhoovered floor?' They were
veering away from his mother—which seemed fine
by both of them.

'Hoovering's good for the soul.'

His mouth twitched. Just a little. The beginning
of a smile. 'Do you know how much hair a dog like
Horse will shed?'

'He has to grow some hair back first,' she said
warmly. 'He grows, I'll hoover. We've made a deal.'

'While you've been sitting on the beach, staring
at the moon.'

'It's filling time. How long do you reckon it'll take
him to figure whoever he wants isn't coming?'

'Dogs have been faithful to absent masters for
years.'

'Years?'

'Years.'

'I was hoping maybe another half an hour.'

'Years.'

'Uh-oh.'

'And years.'

'I don't know what else to do,' she whispered.

Her problem. This was her problem, he thought,
and it was only what she deserved, taking on a damaged dog...

As he'd taken on a damaged dog sixteen years
ago and not regretted it once. Until it was over.

He'd had his turn. Yes, this was Nikki's dog, Nikki's problem, but he could help.

'I don't think you're doing anyone any favours by letting him stare at where a boat isn't,' he said.

'I'm doing my best.'

'Yes,' he said. 'I know that.'

She cast him a look that was suspicious to say the least. 'I didn't mean to mess with your mother's memory,' she told him.

'Yeah.' He deserved that, he conceded. Like he'd deserved the hit over the head? But she had her reasons for that. Her heart was in the right place even if it was messing with…his heart?

That was a dumb thing to think, but think it he did. Since Lisbette left…well, maybe even before, a long time before, he'd closed down. Lisbette had whirled into his life, stunned him, ripped him off for all he was worth and whirled out again. He'd been a kid, lonely, naïve and a sitting duck.

He wasn't a sitting duck any longer. He'd closed up. Jem had wriggled her way into his life, he'd loved her and he'd lost her. She'd been the last chink in his armour, and there was no way he was opening more.

But this woman…

She wasn't looking to rip him off as Lisbette had—he knew that. Lisbette, getting up every two hours because she was worried about him? Ha!

Nor was she trying to edge into the cracks around

his heart like Jem had. She might be needy but it was a different type of needy.

It was Nikki and Horse against the world—when she didn't know a blind thing about dogs.

She was blundering. She was a walking disaster but she was a disaster who meant well.

'I overreacted with the wall,' he conceded. 'I looked out and saw you and the dog and that's what I remember most about my mother. Her sitting for hour after hour, sorting stones. She did it everywhere. She and Billy.'

'Billy?'

'She had a collie. He seemed old as long as I can remember. He pined when she died, and my dad shot him.'

'He shot him?' She sounded appalled.

'He was never going to get over Mum's death.'

'You were how old?'

'Eight.'

'You lost your mum, and your dad shot her dog?'

How to say it? The day of the funeral, coming home, Billy whining, his father saying, 'Get to your room, boy.' A single shot.

He didn't have to tell her. She touched his hand and the horror of that day was in her touch.

'And I hit you over the head,' she whispered. 'And Henrietta said your wife left you. And your own dog died. If I were you I'd have crawled into a nice comfy psychiatric ward and thought up a diagnosis that'd keep me there for the rest of my life. Instead...'

'How did we get here?' He had no idea. One minute this woman was irritating the heck out of him, the next she was putting together stuff he didn't think about; didn't want to think about. This was his place, his beach. He'd come down here for a quiet think, and here he was being psychoanalysed.

He felt exposed.

It was a weird thing to think. She hadn't said anything that wasn't common knowledge but it was as if she could see things differently.

She had her arm round Horse's neck and she was tugging him close, and all of a sudden he felt a jolt, like what would it feel to be in the dog's place?

The dog whined. Stupid dog.

'You want dog lessons,' he said, more roughly than he intended.

'Horse doesn't need lessons. He's smart.'

'He's staring at an empty sea,' he said.

'He's devoted. He'll get over it. Needs must.'

'Says you who's still pining for your creepy boss.'

'I'm trying to get over it,' she said with dignity. 'I'm not sitting on the beach wailing. I'm doing my best. Don't we all?'

She rose and brushed sand from the back of her trousers. With his collar released, Horse took a tentative step towards the sea. Nikki's hand hit the collar at the same time as his did. Their fingers touched.

Flinched a little but didn't let go. Settled beside each other, a tiny touch but unnerving.

Settling.

Things were settling for him. He wasn't sure why.

Maybe it was watching her reaction to what he'd told her tonight, added to what he knew local gossip would have told her. His mother's death, his father, Lisbette, his mother's dog and Jem… Her reaction seemed to validate stuff he tried not to think about.

Permission to feel sorry for himself?

Permission to move on.

Towards Nikki? Towards yet another disaster?

Not in a million years. He'd spent all his life being taught that solitary was safe. He wasn't about to change that now.

But he could help her. It was the least he could do.

'Horse needs a master,' he told her.

'He's only got me,' she said defensively. 'Why are we being sexist? A master?'

'I mean,' he said patiently, 'a pack leader. He's lost his. He's looking for him; if he can't find him he needs a new one.'

'Right,' she said. 'Pack leader. Can I buy one at the Banksia Bay Co-op?'

He grinned. His hand was still touching hers. He should pull it away but he didn't. Things were chang-ing—had changed. There was something about the night, the moonlight on the water, the big needy dog between them…

There was something about her expression. She was sounding defiant, braving it out, but things were rotten in this woman's world as well. Nikki and Horse, both needy to the point of desperation.

That need had nothing to do with him. He should pull away—but he didn't.

'Attitude,' he said, deciding he'd be decisive, and she blinked.

'Pack leader attitude?'

'That's it. So who decided to come down the beach, you or Horse?'

'He was miserable.' She sounded defensive.

'So you followed.'

'I held onto him. He would have run.'

'But he walked in front, yes? Team leaders walk in front. The pack's at the back.'

'You're saying I need to growl at him? Make him subservient? He's already miserable.'

'He'll be miserable until you order him not to be, and he decides you're worth swapping loyalty.'

'I shouldn't have let him come down to the beach?'

'There's not a lot of point being down here, is there?' he said, gentler as he watched her face. And Horse's face. He could swear the dog was listening, his great eyes pools of despair. 'He's been dumped by a low-life. How's it going to make him feel better to stare at an empty sea? It's up to you to take his place.'

'The low-life's place?'

'That's the one.'

'I haven't had much practice at being the low-life,' she said. 'I'm a follower. Dumb and dumber, that's me.'

'We're not talking about your love life.'

'We're not?'

'That's shrink territory, not mine.'

'Like your stone wall.'

'Do you mind?'

'Butt out?' She sighed and tried for a smile. 'Fine. Consider me butted. What do I need to be a pack leader? A whip? Leathers?'

'Discipline.'

She grinned. 'Really? Don't tell me, stockings and garters as well.'

He stared at her in the moonlight and he couldn't believe it. She was laughing. Laughing!

The tension of the night dissipated, just like that. Except…a sudden vision of Nikki in stockings and garters…

He almost blushed.

'I mean,' he said, trying to stop the corners of his mouth twitching, 'you tell Horse what you expect and you follow through. He's hungry? Use it. Call him, reward him when he comes. Teach him to sit, stay, the usual dog things. But mostly teach him no.

He's galloping towards you with a road in between; you need to hold your hand up, yell no and have him stop in his tracks. The same with coming down here. You can bring him down here on your terms, with a ball, something to do to keep him occupied. The minute he stares out to sea like he's considering the low-life, then that's a no. Hard, fast and mean it.'

'You're good at training dogs?'

'I had a great dog. Smart as Einstein. She trained me.'

'I'm sure Horse is smart.'

'Prove it.'

'I'm not sure…'

'Henrietta's daughter takes personal dog coaching. I'm amazed Henrietta hasn't introduced you already.'

'Henrietta left a card,' she conceded.

'There you go.'

'You're not interested in helping yourself?'

'No.' Hard. Definite. He watched her face close and regretted it, but couldn't pull it back.

'I'm not scary,' she said, almost defiantly, and he thought what a wuss—was he so obvious?

'I'm busy,' he said. 'This is the first full day I haven't worked since…'

'Since Jem died?'

'Nikki…'

'I know.' She tugged Horse towards her a little, which forced his hand to let go of the collar. Which meant they were no longer touching. 'You want me to butt out. Respect your boundaries. I've been respecting boundaries for years. You'd think I'd be good at it.'

'I didn't mean…'

'You know, I'm very sure you did,' she told him. 'Tell me what to do.'

'What do you mean?'

'With Horse,' she said patiently. 'Training. What should I do first?'

'Take his collar and say "Come".' This was solid ground. Dog training. He could handle this.

'Come,' she said and tugged and Horse didn't move. Stared rigidly out to sea.

'Come!' Another tug.

Gabe sighed. 'Okay, you're on the head end. We're going to roll him.'

'What?'

'He has to learn to submit, otherwise he'll spend the rest of his life waiting for his low-life. Say "Down".'

'Down.'

'Like you mean it!'

'Down!'

'You sound like a feather duster.'

'I do not.'

'Pretend the boat's sinking. The kid at the other end is standing there with a tin can and a stupid expression. He bails or you drown. Are you going to say "Bail" in that same voice?'

'He's an abandoned dog. He nearly died. He's hurt and confused. You want me to yell at him?'

'He's hurt and confused and he needs to relax. The only way he can relax is if he thinks someone else is in charge. You.'

'You do it.'

'I'm not his pack leader. Do it, Nikki, or you'll have him howling at the door for weeks, killing himself with exhaustion. You say "Down" like you mean it and we bring him down.'

'I don't…'

'Just do it.'

'Down,' she snapped in a voice so full of authority that both Gabe and the dog started. But he had the dog's back legs and Nikki had his collar. Gabe hauled his legs from under him and rolled him before Horse knew what had hit him.

The big dog was on his back. Shocked into submission.

'Tell him he's a good dog but keep him down,' Gabe said.

'This is cruel. He's not fit…'

'He's going to pine until we do it. Do it.'

'G… Good dog.'

'Now let him up again.'

The dog lumbered to his feet.

'Now down again.'

'Down!'

Once again Gabe pushed his legs from under him. The dog folded.

'Good dog,' Nikki said, holding him down and the dog's tail gave a tentative, subjugated wag.

'Once more.'

'Down!' And this time Gabe didn't have to push. The dog crouched and rolled with only a slight push and pull from Nikki.

'Good dog. Great,' Nikki said and her voice wobbled.

The dog stood again, unsure, but this time he moved imperceptibly to Nikki's side. He looked up at her instead of out to sea.

'Now tell him to come and tug,' Gabe said, and Nikki did and the big dog moved docilely up the beach by her side.

'Good dog,' Nikki said and sniffed.

'Why are you crying?'

'I'm not.'

'You're allergic to command?'

'I'm not built to be a sergeant major.'

'Horse needs a sergeant major,' he said as he fell in beside her. 'You are what you have to be. Like me being owner of half a dozen boats, employing crews.'

'You don't like that?'

They were walking up the track, Nikki with Horse beside her, Gabe with his hand hovering, just in case

Horse made a break for it. But Horse was totally submissive. He was probably relieved. He'd spent too long as it was waiting for his scumbag owner. He needed a new one.

There were parallels. Caring for Horse...

Taking on this town's fishing fleet.

Nikki was waiting for an answer. Not pushing. Just walking steadily up the track with her dog.

She was a peaceful woman, he thought. Self contained. Maybe she'd had to be.

Why the sniff? Tears?

Ignore them.

'I never saw myself as head of a fleet,' he told her. 'But when the fishing industry round here started to falter I was single with no responsibilities. I'd been away, working on the rigs, making myself some serious money. I could afford to take a few risks. But in the end I didn't need to. Fishing's in my blood and I knew what'd work.'

'But now... You enjoy it?'

'Fishing's my life.'

'It sounds boring.'

'So you do what in your spare time?' he demanded. 'Macramé?

'Dog training,' she said steadily. 'I now have a career and a hobby and a pet. What more could a girl want? What do you have, Gabe Carver?'

'Everything I want.'

They reached the house in silence. Reached the

porch. Nikki opened the door and ushered Horse inside. Hesitated.

'He'll stand at the door and howl,' she said, and he looked at her face and saw the tracks of tears. What had he said to upset her?

'Only if you let him.'

'How do I not let him?'

He sighed. 'Where's he sleeping?'

'In my bedroom.'

'Not on your bed. You're pack leader.'

'I know that much. Besides, the bed's not big enough.'

'So show me.'

She swung open the bedroom door. A bed, single, small. He looked at her in surprise. He hadn't been here when her furniture was delivered so he was seeing this for the first time. It was practically a child's bed.

'You don't like stretching?'

'Not if there's no one to stretch to.'

Silence. There were a million things to say, but suddenly nothing.

The bedroom was chintzy. Pretty pink. Dainty. It made a man nervous just to look at it.

Horse whined and he thought *I'm with you, mate.* To sleep in a bedroom like this…

But at least Horse had a sensible bed. Henrietta knew dogs, and she'd provided a trampoline bed that was almost as big as Nikki's.

'Say "Bed",' he told Nikki.

'Bed.' Horse didn't move an inch.

Gabe sighed. 'Bail the dratted boat.'

'Bed!' That was better. Sergeant major stuff.

Gabe shoved Horse from behind. Horse lumbered up onto the trampoline.

'Say "Down."'

'Down,' Nikki said and the dog rolled.

'Stay,' Nikki said and stepped back and grinned as Horse did just that.

Horse looked up at her and put a tentative paw down onto the floor.

'Stay!' Her best 'bail the boat' voice.

The paw retreated.

'How about that?' Nikki said, her smile widening. 'I'm a pack leader.'

'You'll make a great one.'

'I will,' she said and turned to him. Fast.

She was suddenly a bit too close.

She was suddenly very close.

'Make sure the dog stays there,' he said, a bit too gruffly. They were by the dog's bed, so close they were almost touching. They were by Nikki's bed as well. It was just as well it wasn't his bed, he thought, the wide, firm, king-sized bed he'd bought for himself when he'd come back here to live.

He had a sudden flash of recall. Last night. Nikki tiptoeing in to check he wasn't dead, leaning over him…

He could have…

No.

But she was so close. He turned to go—a man had to make a move—but suddenly she'd taken his hands in hers, tugging him back to face her.

'Thank you,' she said. 'For coming down to the beach to find me.'

'You're welcome.' He hadn't gone down to find her, he thought, but he wasn't thinking clearly and it seemed way too much trouble to explain.

'And I can see why you don't want to get involved. I won't ask you to. I've been a nuisance. But I meant well. I mean well.'

'You do.' Big of him to concede that much.

'And your head really is better?'

'Not hurting at all.' Almost the truth.

She smiled. It was a really cute smile, he thought. He could see the tracks of those unexplained tears and it made her seem cuter. All in all…

All in all, Nikki Morrissy was really cute all over.

'Goodnight,' she said and then, inexplicably, un-accountably, she stood on tiptoe and she kissed him. Lightly, a feather-touch. Maybe she'd even meant it to be an air-kiss but he moved. Maybe he tugged her a bit closer and her lips brushed his.

Burned.

She pulled back, startled. Which was how he felt. Startled.

To say the least.

'Just…thank you,' she said. Struggled for words. Struggled to find something to talk about other than the kiss. 'And…and I'm so sorry your dog died. Jem must have been amazing.'

'She was.'

'You want to tell me about her?' she said but there were limits, even if she was looking at him with eyes that'd melt an iceberg.

She was his tenant. *His tenant.*

He'd helped her as much as he could.

'Goodnight,' he said and backed to the door.

'I didn't mean to kiss you,' she murmured, but he hardly heard her.

A man had to take a stand some time. A man had to know when to retreat.

He retreated.

CHAPTER SIX

THERE was no reason to get up. The sensation was so novel it had Gabe lying in bed at five in the morning thinking the world was off balance.

All but one of his boats were out. They'd left in a group yesterday morning and weren't due back until tomorrow. The one stuck in harbour through lack of crew—the *Lady Nell*—was the one needing least attention. The propeller was checked. The cray-pots were mended.

Even his dratted bookwork was up to date.

He could sleep until midday if he wanted.

He didn't want. His world was out of kilter.

Because of lack of work?

Because of Nikki.

Because she'd kissed him?

Because she'd touched him with her crazy floundering from assertive career woman to a woman who was exposed on all sides.

She'd taken in a dog as big as she was. She'd given

her heart and in doing so… She'd pierced a part of him he'd protected with care for years.

And he didn't want it pierced. He had to close it off again fast, but the fact that she was living right through the wall was enough to do his head in.

He could evict her. Because of the dog?

He was turning into his father.

His window was wide open. From where he lay he could see the gap in the stone fence. He thought of Nikki's face as he'd yelled.

He'd hurt her.

Last night she'd cried and he didn't know why.

The wall was there, looking at him, as it had looked at Nikki.

He climbed out of bed and went to get his mother's books. Went back to bed. He read for an hour.

Looked at the wall.

The thought of picking up those stones, taking up where his mother had left off…

How could he do that?

How could he start again?

His mother. Lisbette. Jem. Pain at every turn.

He thought of the appalling time after Lisbette left. Realising that all she'd said had been lies. Realising the extent of what she'd stolen from him.

After Lisbette, he'd taken Jem and headed west, where his experience landed him a job on a rig supply boat. Jem was included—he was a package deal, employ me, my dog comes too. But it was no problem. Jem loved their life at sea and Gabe was good. Within a year he was captaining his own boat. He could get stuff to the rigs in weather no one else would face.

He worked hard. Crew came and went. Jem was his only constant.

The protective layer he'd built around himself grew thicker. He was okay.

Moving back here… That'd been a risk, but he'd heard stories of the trouble with the fleet. Maybe the loneliness had got to him. It wouldn't hurt to help the people who'd once been good to him; who'd tried in their way to stand between him and his father.

And that was okay, too. By the time he came home the house had lost the worst of its memories. Only the shades of his mother remained.

He'd been able to step in and maintain his distance. He and Jem.

Now, just him.

And Nikki and Horse.

Who made him think of finishing the wall…

He did not need them interfering with his solitary lifestyle.

He tossed the books aside. Pulled on his fishing gear. He'd head to the harbour.

He had to get out of here.

He had to get away from Nikki?

Away from the thought of letting down some of

his carefully built defences. How could a man ever do that? And why would he want to?

Nikki and Horse sat on the wharf, watched the seagulls and watched the early morning sun glinting over the distant sea.

The harbour was deserted. Most of the boats were out. The only ones left were pleasure craft and the tenders used to take owners out to bigger boats at swing moorings.

Swing moorings. Tenders. She smiled to herself. She'd only been here three weeks and already she was learning the local lingo.

'Do you know it already?' she asked Horse. 'Were you a fishing dog?'

Horse was subdued but pliant. He'd woken at first light and whined. Nikki had taken him outside. He'd done what he needed to do and then looked longingly towards the beach.

'No,' Nikki told him in her best Leader-Of-The-Pack voice and hauled him back inside. She cooked bacon and eggs for breakfast and shared. She was fed up with Dinners For One and it was fun to cook for an appreciative appetite. Horse wolfed the bacon and nuzzled her hand in what seemed like gratitude, but then he whined and looked at the door again.

He was torn between two loyalties. Lady with the bacon or the sod who'd abandoned him.

'Choose me,' Nikki said but Horse still whined.

She needed displacement activity.

So here they were, sitting on the jetty, trying not to stare at the only decent boat in port.

Gabe's boat. The *Lady Nell*.

Big and powerful and workmanlike. Like Gabe himself.

He'd made her cry.

Not...not him, she thought. It was the mixture of all sorts of stuff.

For the last two months she'd been caught up in her own drama, her own betrayal. But so much more had happened to Gabe.

He didn't want sympathy. There was no way he'd take it, but the touch of his mouth on hers...

It made her want to take him and hold, tell him the world wasn't such a bad place; there were decent people, people who could love...

He didn't want to hear it. Neither did she.

Was she still in love with Jon?

If Jon appeared in front of her right now, told her his marriage was over, had been over for years, it had all been a misunderstanding, would she go back to him?

It was doing her head in.

She was sitting on the wharf letting her head implode.

It was still really early. Six-thirty. Uncivilised. What was she doing here?

Horse whined and turned and jerked on his lead

and Nikki swivelled to see. Gabe was striding along the jetty.

Dressed for work. Fisherman's overalls with braces. Rubber boots. His shirt sleeves were once more rolled to above the elbow.

Striding purposely towards his boat, seeing her, stopping dead.

'Nikki,' he said in a tone that said she was the last person he wanted here. She flinched but Horse surged forward and was too strong for her to hold. Henrietta had provided her with a choke chain—to be used 'just for the first week or so because he's so big and there's nothing of you'—but there was no way she was using it. So Horse hauled and she followed.

Feeling foolish.

His expression said she ought to hike out of here fast, taking her dog with her.

'H…Hi,' she managed as Horse reached him and attempted to jump. Gabe caught the dog's legs, placed him firmly down.

'Sit,' he growled and Horse sat. 'Hey,' Gabe said, unable to hide pleasure. 'He must have had some training.'

'I'm worried someone's looking for him,' she ventured. It seemed as good a way as any to start a conversation with someone who obviously wanted her somewhere else.

'Henrietta kept him for ten days. Raff, our local

cop, broadcast his details to every cop, to every marine outfit, to every fisherman within two hundred miles up and down the coast. He was found with no collar and evidence of severe neglect. There's no suggestion there of a happy ending.'

'Well, he has one with me,' she snapped, because he was looking at her as if…she was stupid. Dumb for offering this dog a home?

'You can't hold him,' he said mildly and she flushed. Maybe she was reading more into his words than he intended but she was keeping this dog, regardless of what her tough-guy landlord thought.

'Henrietta gave me a choke chain. I tried it on myself. That's exactly what it does—choke. There's no way I'm putting it on Horse.'

'You tried it on yourself…?'

'It's awful. You tug on it, you think you're choking.'

'You only use it while you're training.'

'Did you use one on Jem?'

'I got Jem as a pup. And I'm bigger than you.'

'I do weights,' she said, glaring. 'If I want to stop Horse, I can.'

He nodded. Grinned. Walked the few steps to his boat and leaped aboard. Disappeared into the wheelhouse and came out holding…what?

A chunk of salami.

He walked back to Horse, showed him the sausage, let him sniff, backed off and called. Waving the salami.

'Here, boy. Nice sausage. Come and get it.'

Horse lunged forward.

Nikki held with all the power she possessed and yelled with all the power in her lungs. 'No!'

She wrenched Horse back, then dived in front of him so she was a barrier between dog and sausage. She planted her feet.

'Sit,' she said in a voice she didn't know she had.

Horse sat.

Wow.

She looked down at the dog, at his great goofy desperate-to-please expression, and once again she wanted to cry.

She glanced back at Gabe and caught an expression on his face that was almost similar. 'Wow!' His echo of her thought was so pat she found herself grinning.

'We've been practising all night,' she lied smugly, bending down and hugging Horse. 'Good dog. Great dog.'

She straightened, still grinning—and Horse surged forward to Gabe and grabbed the sausage.

She burst out laughing. Horse wolfed the sausage in two gulps, returned to her side and sat like a benign angel. Obedience personified.

'I think I'm in love,' Nikki said and knew she was.

'You've made a good start,' Gabe conceded.

'I…are you going fishing?' Stupid question. He was dressed for fishing.

'Just checking pots.'

'Pots?'

'I have cray-pots laid along the coast. I don't have a crew but I can do that myself.'

'You're taking your boat out by yourself?'

'Yes.' He swung himself on board and unlocked the wheelhouse. 'I'll be back this afternoon.'

'What about your head?'

'It's fine.'

'I read on the Internet. Forty-eight hours after concussion…'

'You're not still expecting me to drop dead?'

'I keep feeling that crunch,' she said miserably. 'And the side of your face looks awful.'

It did, he conceded. He'd looked in the mirror to shave and pretty near died of fright.

'I'm fine,' he said.

'Please don't go fishing alone.'

What else was he expected to do? 'There's no one else to go fishing with,' he said explosively. 'Since you sent the rest of my crew out without me.'

'I meant it for the best. You can't go out.'

'You're going to stop me how?'

She took a deep breath. She collared Horse and she tugged him forward.

Horse reacted almost too well. He leapt the gap between wharf and boat, and Nikki was hauled after.

She caught her foot on the safety line and sprawled. Gabe reached her before she slid into the water. Tugged her up so she was standing on the deck beside him.

Held her.

'What sort of crazy stunt…? You could drown yourself.'

'I'm an excellent swimmer,' she managed, gasping, hauling herself back from him. She felt winded and stupid, and the feel of those arms… They had a girl thoroughly discombobulated. 'And if I hadn't fallen over Horse…'

'Anyone would fall over Horse,' he said grimly, and turned to see Horse heading along to the bow, standing there like a figurehead on a bowsprit. Any minute now he'd raise one paw and lean into the wind.

'He's used to boats,' he said.

'He needs to be used to boats,' she said. 'We're staying on board until you see sense. Your crew will be back tomorrow. It won't kill you to stay on land.'

'I want to check my cray-pots.'

'Then take someone with you.'

He glared. She crossed her arms and jutted her jaw. Tree-hugger chaining herself to a mighty oak. Or ship.

He sighed. He slipped into the wheelhouse and started the engine. Strode aft and released the rear stay. Strode forward—and their connection to the wharf was gone.

She gasped. 'What…?'

'You want me to have company?' Gabe snapped. 'Fine. Make yourself at home and stay out of my way.'

When tree-huggers chained themselves to trees they didn't expect their trees to get up and walk. Or get up and sail out of the harbour.

Uh-oh. Uh-oh, uh-oh, uh-oh.

There was a twenty-yard gap between wharf and boat. Should she jump off and swim for it?

Dragging Horse behind her?

Horse was still doing his merman impersonation at the bow. His nose was pointing into the wind, every sense quivering.

Yesterday he'd looked half dead. Now…he almost looked beautiful. If you looked past the mangy coat.

Coat.

She was wearing a light pullover. Cotton. She glanced at Gabe, who was intent behind the wheel, ignoring her. He was in his weatherproofs, dressed for work.

Her pullover was pale pink. Her jeans were a soft blue.

She was wearing her Gucci loafers.

Hardly fishing gear.

'There's a jetty at the harbour mouth,' Gabe

growled, seemingly intent on keeping the wheel steady. 'I'll put you off there.'

'You've done this to frighten me.'

'I've done this because I have work to do,' he snapped. 'You're in the way.'

'I'm not in the way,' she muttered. 'It's a big boat.'

'You don't seriously want to come to sea with me?'

Deep breath. Resolution. 'If you're stupid enough to want to take the boat out by yourself, then yes, I do,' she said. 'It was me who hit you. I feel responsible. If someone else hit you, you'd be welcome to be as stupid as you want. I wouldn't care.'

'You don't have to care.'

'I told you. I hit you, I don't have a choice.'

'Get off at the jetty.'

'No.' Back to tree-hugging. She was not, however, sounding as sure as she might have been.

'You'll get seasick.'

There was a thought. Hmm.

She'd been on a couple of cruises with her parents. One with Jon. 'I don't get seasick.' Or sometimes, just a little.

'We're going around reefs, checking pots in rough water. Have you ever been on a small boat in rough water?'

'I don't care,' she burst out. 'It's you who's being stubborn and ridiculous and a totally dumb, masochistic male. Your call. If you go out, you take me with you, seasick or not.'

'Fine,' he said and shifted the wheel so instead of pointing to the jetty at the harbour mouth they were pointing to the open sea.

Um…what had she done?

She kept her arms crossed and felt stupid.

The sea breeze wasn't all that warm.

They hit cross waves at the harbour entrance and she had to uncross her arms to hold on. Whoa, cruise liners never rocked like this.

'Nikki?'

'What?' She was glowering. Trying to stay righteous and purposeful.

'Put these on.' They were clear of the harbour mouth and he'd left the wheel for a moment. He took the couple of steps to where she stood and handed her a coat even more disgusting than his.

'I'm not sure…'

'Put it on,' he growled. 'And the life jacket with it. There's a packet of seasick pills on the bench below. Take one. Then tie a safety line to Horse. Then you can watch for signs of concussion all you want, as long as you stay out of my way.'

It took half an hour to reach the reef where he'd set the cray-pots. For all that time Nikki sat in the bow, holding onto Horse.

She was right in his line of vision, a slight figure

in a battered coat way too big for her, with Horse draped over her knees. Both of them were gazing into the wind. Horse's ears flopped about in the breeze.

Nikki's hair practically had a life of its own.

She had a pert bob, cut to sculptural perfection. It was smooth and glossy and lovely—or it had been until the first burst of spray flew over the bow.

Her hair sort of forgot about being smooth. It kinked a bit.

He watched, fascinated, as the spray and the wind did their worst. By the time they were halfway to their destination her hair was a mass of curls. She no longer looked like a smooth, professional city woman. She was enveloped in a coat liberally embellished with fish scales, her hair was a riot and she was draped in a huge dog.

She hadn't succumbed to seasickness. On the contrary, once she'd settled, once she'd forgotten to glower, she almost looked as if she was enjoying herself. When she was hit by spray she turned her face into it, even laughed. She hugged her dog, and Horse looked pretty happy, too.

She'd forgotten she was checking him for concussion, or maybe she figured as long as the boat was on course she didn't need to. She was simply enjoying the ride and Gabe, who'd practically kidnapped her, felt a pang of...

Of something he didn't know how to handle. He'd

brought her with him because he was frustrated and angry and he'd wanted to teach her a lesson. *Stay out of my life.*

Now she was in his life even more, and it was making him feel…

He didn't know how it was making him feel. As if he wanted to turn the boat round and head back for harbour, dump her and run?

Yeah, as if that was a sensible thing to do.

Her hair was amazing.

'Gabe!'

She was on her feet, yelling to him. 'Gabe!'

He pulled back the throttle, alarmed, and swung out of the wheelhouse to see.

Seals.

He'd been too busy watching her, watching her crazy hair, to notice, and he didn't look for seals anyway. It wasn't that he didn't like seeing them—he did, apart from when they were after his fish—but there was a massive seal colony on a rocky island a couple of miles south of Banksia Bay, and seals were simply part and parcel of his life.

They weren't part and parcel of Nikki's life. She was gazing down at them in awe.

They were riding his bow wave.

They truly were wonderful, he conceded, trying to see them as Nikki must be seeing them. These were pups, half grown, still mostly fed by their parents so they were here to have fun. The bow wave and the wake made by the *Lady Nell* were just right for them to surf. There were dozens of them, streaming in and out of the waves, riding alongside the boat, surging ahead and slipping behind. Leaping up, leaping over each other, simply having fun. Nikki was holding the rail and gasping with pleasure.

An old bull seal pulled out of the wave, reared back, surged on ahead.

Gabe grinned. He knew this guy. Mostly the bull seals held themselves apart, but this old guy had lost his harem long since. Instead of moping alone, he'd decided to relive his youth.

He slipped back into the wheelhouse, pushed the throttle back to full power and went out again. The seals practically whooped with joy at the bigger bow wave.

'They're tame,' Nikki whispered, awed.

'Not them. They're wild and free. They know what they want from me, though. Decent surf.'

'They're magnificent. Oh…' One of the young ones, smaller than the rest, surged up, leaped right out of the water ahead of the wave, then sank out of sight. If she'd reached out she could have touched him.

She was clutching Gabe's arm, gazing down with pure delight. 'Oh…'

'They eat my fish,' Gabe growled but his heart wasn't in it. He was watching her. Where was his sleek, perfectly groomed tenant now? She was in a battered, fishing sou'wester. Her hair was a mass of tangled curls, getting more and more wild as the spray soaked her. A sliver of mascara had smudged down her cheek.

He had this really strong urge…

A wave hit them broadside, not so big to worry him—he'd never have left the wheelhouse if there was a possibility of a big sea—but it was big enough to make Nikki stagger and clutch.

He let her clutch. His arm came round her waist and held—and she didn't appear to notice.

She was totally absorbed in the seals, in the antics of the pups. They were born clowns. It was as if they were putting on their own personal show, with the old bull seal trying valiantly to keep up.

The pups were jumping the bull seal, darting round his massive body as if he was a rock and they were playing tag around him.

'He's huge,' Nikki whispered.

'Cecil. He's a local legend. He's the only seal in the known world who runs his own playgroup. Most bull seals when they're past their prime head for a lone rock and live out the rest of their lives sulking. Cecil thinks this is a great alternative.'

She chuckled, a lovely throaty chuckle that made something kick inside Gabe's gut. Something he wasn't sure how to handle.

His arm was still around her. She was nestled

against him, watching the seals. Her eyes were alight with laughter, her body curved against him as if this was the most natural position in the world.

He wanted, quite badly, to kiss her.

Very badly.

Defences? Why would a man want defences?

'Nikki...'

But right at that moment one of the pups leapt up and twisted right next to where they stood, so close it almost brushed Horse's nose.

Horse had been staring over the side with bemusement, not sure what he should do in this situation.

This, however, called for action. There were some things which a mature dog should not put up with, and cheeky pups taunting him was obviously one of them.

He crouched under the side rail so he was leaning right over the side and he barked, a massive, throaty bark that said, *Oi, enough—this is my territory; you guys know your place.*

Nikki chuckled and stooped to hug him, and Gabe felt her leave his side with a wrench of loss.

Given the choice, he wouldn't have let her go.

'Hey, it's okay, they're having fun,' Nikki told Horse, and Horse wagged his tail, practically beaming, and crouched again and went back to barking.

The seals backed away a little, darted out, darted back, started leaping again.

It seemed Horse was no threat.

Horse barked on, fit to wake the dead.

'Tell him "No" or he'll deafen us,' Gabe said, half laughing himself, but still with that wrenching feeling of loss.

'No!' Nikki said and then raised her voice. 'No!' Horse subsided.

Nikki looked smug.

He wanted to kiss her so badly...

Another wave hit them broadside and the boat rolled. He reached to steady Nikki but she'd already clutched the rail. She was fine.

They were nearing the reef; the waves were building. He needed to head back into the wheelhouse and leave Nikki to Horse and to her seals.

He did, but it was a wrench.

The desire to kiss her went with him.

He pulled up twenty cray-pots and felt as if he'd done a decent morning's work. The hold was now full of live crays. Good, big ones.

Maybe he'd cook one for dinner, invite Nikki over.

Was he out of his mind?

But a man could think about it. Resolutions were made to be broken. How long since he'd invited a woman out?

She was his tenant. It was asking for trouble.

She was adorable.

That was asking for more trouble.

She'd insisted on helping and, to his astonishment,

she really could help. He explained the winch system once, and she got it straight away. It was hard winching in cray-pots by himself. The pots were set in shallow water at the back of a low-lying reef. The boat had to be held steady or they'd end up on the rocks. If he'd been working by himself it was a matter of watching the sea, then heading in during a glimmer of calm, hooking the pot and winching it up from back in the wheelhouse while he could watch the sea as it came up. Then get back to safe water before he could swing the pot over the side.

But Nikki got it. She watched him do one, she demanded to try, she hooked the second on the third run—not bad for an amateur—and she hauled the pot in by herself.

Horse objected to the weird crustaceans in the traps but he only barked once. 'No,' Nikki said and the big dog subsided and watched.

He had a crew, he thought. A woman and a dog.

He thought of the morning he'd have had if she hadn't come, and he thought why had he not wanted to take her? She lit his day.

There was a dangerous thought.

Why was it dangerous?

With the last pot was lifted he headed back from the dangerous waters of the reef,

The water out here was calm. Nikki had untied Horse—they'd needed Horse's spot to stack the pots while they worked and he seemed settled. With the pots all emptied, woman and dog were back to watching the seal pups. Nikki was hugging Horse. She was smiling at Horse. She was smiling at the pups.

She was smiling at him.

It felt…

Dangerous.

Insidious in its sweetness.

Why was he so nervous?

Because his gut said this was a woman who had the power to mess with his equanimity.

Was equanimity such a big deal anyway?

All his life he'd been a loner, except…

Yeah, except for his mother. She'd loved him. She'd held him, cuddled him, stood between him and his brute of a father.

Left him. Not her fault, though. There was no word bad enough to describe cancer.

Lisbette. Held him, loved him, ripped him off for everything he was worth.

He'd thought he was in love. How did a man recover trust in his judgement after that?

He didn't. Why should he? Was it worth the risk?

Jem. Dogs.

Back in the wheelhouse, he glanced out at Horse and Nikki, and he thought big dogs and short life-spans. Nikki was giving her heart to a dog, and in a few short years she'd have the heart ripped out of her.

She was laughing now, watching Horse watch a couple of gulls swooping overhead. Horse was trying to figure whether they were a threat. Putting his paws over his head in case they were.

When she lost Horse she'd stop laughing.

He could be there…

Where was he going with this?

Back to port. He gunned the motor, pushing the revs, deciding he needed to be back on dry land fast. Thinking he needed to get his head together fast. Then he noticed a boat on the horizon, coming fast. Much faster than his boat.

It was a pleasure craft, he saw, as the distance between them grew smaller. A couple of yahoo guys were speeding for the sake of it, gunning their flimsy fibreglass craft to the limit. Using gas for the sake of it. Thrill-seeking. They wouldn't even see the seals, he thought, or anything else. They were only intent on speed.

They veered nearer, stupidly close, probably trying to catch his bow wave to give them a more exciting ride. They yelled and waved and veered in and out of his wake. They did a three-sixty degree turn—and then they were gone, speeding into the distance.

And before he realised what was happening…

Horse gave a long, low howl, he lurched out of Nikki's arms, out of her hold and he headed over the side of the boat and after them.

CHAPTER SEVEN

No.

'Horse!' Nikki screamed, hauled off her sou'wester, kicked off her shoes and, before Gabe could react, she was over the side and after him.

No!

They were in seal territory. Pup's playground.

Shark country.

His heart hit his boots as he hauled the boat around, headed out on deck, threw lifebuoys. His gut reaction was to jump straight in after them but a fat lot of use that would be. Three of them in the water while the boat drifted to the reef… He needed to manoeuvre his way to them fast.

He headed back to the wheel. Tried to see.

Horse was a hundred yards from the boat already. Nikki was half the distance but she was heading after him, swimming strongly.

At least she could swim.

She had a life vest on, two bars across her shoul-

ders to be inflated with the pull of a cord. He should
be grateful she hadn't pulled it off with her jacket.

She hadn't pulled the cord. She was intent on
reaching the dog—who was intent on reaching the
speedboat.

Which was now practically out of sight.

'Nikki, head for the lifebuoy,' he yelled, his voice
hoarse with panic, but she was still heading for the
dog.

Stupid, stupid, stupid.

Panic would achieve nothing. Stay cool. Think.

He gunned the boat, heading after her. He cut her
off from the dog and hit neutral.

'I can reach him,' she yelled, changing direction
to go round the boat.

'*We* can reach him,' he yelled back. 'Get back in
the boat. Now!' He hauled one of the buoys back into
the boat and threw it again so it was just in front of
her. 'Hold on and I'll pull.'

'Let me go. I can…'

'Get back in the boat or I'll cosh you with the gaff
and drag you in.' And he meant it.

They were in seal pup territory. Great White
Sharks fed round here, cruising the waters for easy
pickings. Pickings like injured seals. The locals
knew never to dive near the seal colony. A human
in the water, creating a splash, looked just like an
injured seal.

He knew the dangers. She didn't. She had to get out of there.

'Horse...' she yelled, sounding desperate. Not as desperate as him.

'We'll get him.' He couldn't manoeuvre the boat closer. It was too big; he risked her being sucked under the propeller. 'Grab the buoy. Now! I mean it, Nikki. Get back on the boat.'

She cast him a look that was half fearful, half angry—and grabbed the buoy.

He hauled her to the side in seconds. Reached down and pulled.

Tugging a grown woman from the sea was no easy task—he'd had guys go overboard before and he'd had to use a harness. Not Nikki. They said women could lift the weight of a car if their child was trapped underneath—that was what this felt like. He lifted her straight up, clinging to the life-buoy, and he didn't even feel her weight.

He felt nothing until she was on the deck, all of her, whole, fine, safe.

'Horse...' For a nanosecond she clung but she was already pulling away, swivelling to search. 'Horse...'

She was in love already, he thought. She loved the great mangy mutt who was swimming steadily to the horizon.

How...?

'We use the lifeboat,' he snapped. 'There's no way he'll cling to a lifebuoy and we won't be able to grab and lift him from this height. I'm gunning the boat to cut him off. Get up on top of the wheelhouse, haul the ties off and slide the lifeboat down to the foredeck. Go!'

He was back at the wheel, hauling the boat round so he was heading out past Horse. Veering round him in a wide arc. Heading to a spot between the dog and where the speedboat had headed.

So Horse would be forced to swim past.

The sick feeling in his gut was growing with every moment. He knew the odds. He'd seen sharks here before. Often. Please...

At least Nikki was safe.

She wouldn't thank him if he didn't get the stupid dog.

Only the dog wasn't stupid, he conceded, as he manoeuvred the boat into position and hit the winch controlling the anchor. The dog was crazily devoted, still loyal to the low-life who'd abandoned him. He was somehow associating the speedboat, the thrill-riding idiots, with his previous owner. He was desperate to find those he'd given his heart to.

Giving your heart... It was the way to destroy yourself.

The lifeboat slipped down over the glass in front of him onto the deck. Nikki clambered down after, water streaming from her soaked clothes, her dripping hair. She seemed almost calm, carefully, sensibly, avoiding blocking his view as she clambered down. She steadied the life-raft on the deck and started unhooking the cleats of the metal stays that formed the side rails.

Woman with sense. Woman who'd just jumped into the midst of a seal colony. Where White Pointers fed…

Any minute…any minute…

He had the boat in position. The dog was swimming towards them now, starting to veer because the *Lady Nell* was in his path.

Drop the anchor.

The anchor struck and held. But it wasn't deep enough for safety; the waves were short and sharp and threatening to break.

'Nikki,' he yelled. 'Come here!'

She cast him a fearful glance, not wanting to let go of the life-raft.

'Here!' he yelled in a voice that matched her dog training voice, and she abandoned the life-raft and headed to the wheel.

'Anchor chain,' he snapped, pointing to the lever that attached to the control. 'Gears. Throttle. Watch the sea.'

'I'm going after…'

'You don't know how to manage the motor on the life-raft and you don't have the strength to haul a dog up. You watch the sea. Every moment. Not me. Not the dog. The sea. I mean it, Nikki, all our lives depend on it. Watch from the east. You see any big sea coming, anything at all, you haul the chain up, wait five seconds, no longer, just so the anchor's clear, then shove her into first gear like this, and turn her nose into the wave. You take action before you need to. Any suspicion of a decent wave, you turn her. Ride the wave, then drop back into neutral, drop the anchor again.'

'Should I just keep her in first gear?'

'No.' Because she couldn't watch the depth sounder, watch the dog, watch the sea all at once, and he didn't want to end up on the rocks. Lowering and raising the anchor was the best way to keep her in position. But he didn't have time to say it. He was already out on deck, lowering the life-raft and slipping down into it.

She saw him slip over the side and then she turned to watch the sea. The waves were coming from the far side of the *Lady Nell* to where Gabe was steering the little boat towards Horse.

Watch the sea. Do not watch Gabe.

She could just glance. Tiny glances in between fierce concentration. A wave was building; she saw the swell further out.

Up with the anchor, into first gear, nose into the wave.

Up and over.

The sea calmed again. Neutral. Drop the anchor. Another glance.

He was almost there, almost to Horse. The swells were pushing Horse inshore; he was almost to the reef. Gabe was manoeuvring at the back of waves that were threatening to flip his tiny craft.

Watch the sea.

Gabe. Horse.

She'd forgotten to breathe.

The seals had disappeared. Dear God, the seals were gone.

He knew what that meant.

He was closing in on Horse but the dog was veering away, sensing that Gabe was intent on stopping him.

'Horse!' He cut the motor so it hardly purred, keeping just enough revs to hold the little craft on course. He was calling in a voice he was struggling to keep calm. 'Come on, boy.'

The dog veered sharply away.

A wave hit broadside. Gabe did a one-eighty, the wave almost tipped—and boat and dog collided.

He had his hand under the dog's collar before they were down the other side of the wave; before Horse could realise what was happening.

Now pull.

The life-raft was soft sided, industrial strength rubber. If Horse fought… He could tear the craft apart.

Where were the seals? What was happening under the surface?

Don't think. Just do.

He grabbed the collar with both hands, leaned backward so that if the dog came he'd end up full length on the floor rather than lurching out of the other side.

Pulled with all his strength.

The dog hauled back. Fought him.

Where were the seals?

He flicked a glance sideways. Nothing. Calm water. Not a seal.

'Come,' he yelled, and he roared the word, a deep, harsh yell that sounded out over the reef to the land beyond. It startled the dog into stillness.

He had an instant only. He hauled as he'd never hauled before.

And the dog came, lurching up and sliding in, toppling over the top of him so he was lying full length in the back of the life-raft with a mass of quivering, sodden dog on top of him.

He had him. He was in the boat!

Look back to the sea, Nikki told herself. Concentrate on the sea.

She sniffed.

Stupid salt water. How did it get to be streaming down her face when she was in the wheelhouse?

* * *

It wasn't over yet.

Luckily, once Gabe had him, Horse ceased to struggle. Maybe it was because the speedboat was out of sight and he knew it wasn't worth it. Or maybe it was because Gabe's hand on his collar was implacable.

'You want to be shark meat? You want me to have to explain that to Nikki?'

Maybe the dog understood. Maybe he didn't. Either way, he submitted as Gabe reached the *Lady Nell*, roped the dinghy to the side, tried to figure how to get him up.

Figured he couldn't. Not here.

Nikki was still watching the sea. He'd half expected her to emerge from the wheelhouse as he approached but she had the sense to stay where she was.

She was, it seemed, calm in a crisis. Apart from jumping into shark-infested water.

'Anchor up, into first gear, nose her out into deep water. Head straight into the waves rather than broadside,' he yelled. 'Slow and steady, because we're tied to the side.'

And she did it, amazingly well for a landlubber, nosing the big boat carefully out, heading into the swells, changing course so no waves caught her broadside, which might have risked jerking the lifeboat, tossing him and Horse into the sea.

Still he saw no seals. He knew what that meant.

There was no use telling Nikki that, though. She had enough to think about.

And finally they were out past the sharp inshore swells, to where the sea flattened into long, low rolls.

'Enough?' she yelled.

'Great. Anchor and help me.' He couldn't climb aboard to get what he needed, because he didn't trust Horse not to lurch over the side again and head for the horizon.

But Nikki was there, following instructions. He roped Horse, looping stays under his midriff, rear and aft, tying his collar, using rope work to fashion a sling.

Once secured, he swung himself up on board the *Lady Nell*, hooked the sling to the cray-pot winch, put the gears into motion.

Instead of a cray-pot being hauled up, a dog.

Nikki caught Horse's head as he reached the top, he looped his arms around the dog's back legs and they hauled him over the side, kneeling, tugging backwards, ending up a tangle of man, woman, dog and sea water.

And laughter. Nikki was laughing. Crying a little too, but hugging her dog as if he was the most wonderful thing she'd ever seen.

And then, because they were lying flat on the deck, side by side, under the dog, she was suddenly hugging him. Tight.

'Oh, Gabe…thank you. You were wonderful. Just wonderful.'

She turned, just a little so she could see him, but he moved at the same time, not intentionally, he'd swear, but it didn't matter because they were nose to nose. She was holding him, her eyes were inches from his, her mouth was just…there…

He kissed her. Of course he kissed her; a man would have to be inhuman not to.

She was streaming sea water. Her curls were dripping and wild. She looked like a drowned rat, only of course it was a ridiculous analogy because her eyes were huge and glowing, and her mouth was soft and full, and…and…

His mouth met hers and the world stilled.

She was cold and shivery and shocked.

She was warm and yielding and wonderful.

She'd been laughing, and for a moment the kiss was an extension of that laughter. An extension of the joy. He felt it blaze between them—shared triumph, awe of what they'd achieved, an extension of drama, shock, fear.

But only for a moment because, as his mouth met hers, things changed. Dissolved. Turned to something else entirely in the power of the link between them.

Heat.

It was like an electric current jolting between them, forging a link, surging with a power so great it threatened to overwhelm him. Her lips were full and tender and yielding, and they felt as if they were melting to him, fire to fire, merging to be part of him, a part he hadn't known was missing until this moment. A part of his whole.

She'd turned to hug him and her arms were around him, holding him close. They were lying almost full length on the deck. Horse was draped over their legs, soaking them. The boat was riding up and down at anchor and all he could feel, all he could sense, all he could focus on, was her lips.

Her mouth.

Nikki.

His arms came around her, tugging her to him as naturally as joining two pieces of a puzzle, setting two pieces where they belonged and feeling the rightness of it.

She was wearing a light sweater. The fabric seemed to have almost disappeared in the wet; he could feel the wonder of her body underneath, the soft, luscious contours of her breasts, the way her body yielded, melted, crushed against him.

Against his sou'wester. Against his fishing gear. He was holding a woman who wore almost nothing and he was dressed for wet weather. He hardly noticed except he wanted her closer, closer and his clothes were getting in the way.

Her mouth...

Nikki.

He'd never felt like this. He'd never known he could feel like this. He had everything he wanted in his life right here, right now.

Stupid? Maybe it was, but there was no way he was going to think that; there was no way he was thinking anything while she was kissing him.

Her hands were in his hair, tugging him closer, deepening the kiss. She wanted this as much as he did. It was as if a key deep within had been turned, releasing emotion he hardly knew he'd locked away. He let himself kiss, he let himself be kissed, and a well of bitterness was unleashed, flowed outward, away and disappeared into the warm salt spray over the ocean.

Nikki...

And then Horse barked.

The dog had been lying limp over their legs, a dead weight neither of them noticed, but when a dog Horse's size barked from your knees and stood and headed for the side again it was time to stop kissing and pay attention.

No matter how much it hurt. No matter that it was a wrench that almost tore him apart.

But he moved. He caught Horse's collar and held. Horse was still attached to the harness but he wasn't taking any chances. Nikki tried to help. She looked as if she was struggling back from somewhere she hadn't known existed. Her eyes held wonder.

Wonder for both of them?

Horse barked again and hauled to the side. Then whined. Gabe tugged him back and looked to see what Horse was barking at.

Something floated to the surface in a pool of crimson.

A seal. Sliced neatly, horribly, in half.

There was a flash of streamlined silver and the thing was gone, hauled down, out of sight, with only the pool of blood remaining.

Nikki's face lost all its colour. He grabbed her as well as Horse, scared she'd faint. He hadn't put the side lines back up; there was no way he was risking her falling.

He had the dog in one hand. His other arm was holding Nikki while she stared in appalled fascination at the disappearing streaks of blood.

'What...what...?' She choked on the words as if she was having trouble breathing. 'It was a seal. What...?'

'A White Pointer,' he said grimly, holding her fast. Trying not to think how close they'd come.

'A White...'

'Sharks,' he said. 'This is seal territory and sharks eat seals.'

'I could have...Horse...'

'That's why I was yelling,' he told her. It was no use lying. She lived here now. If she told anyone about Horse's escapade she'd be told about the sharks. 'Any injured seal is fair game. Sharks sense them by thrashing. Seals are sleek in the water. You guys were asking for trouble.' He motioned to the bloodstained water. 'The shark will be here because of you. He'll have circled for a bit, watched, and then I hauled his supper out of reach. So the seal was the alternative.'

'Oh…' she gasped, and choked back a sob of pure terror, then tugged away from him and stared at him in horror. 'You let me jump over the side.'

'I hardly…'

'You could have yelled "Shark".' *She* was yelling.

'You might have drowned with fright.'

'You could have…'

'What? Yell *Shark*, but nice harmless shark with no teeth? Pat-a-shark territory. Oh, but get out anyway because you might be allergic.'

She choked on something that was half laughter, half shock, then stared again down to where the streaks of blood were now dissipating, leaving a faint crimson tinge to the sea. She shuddered.

Horse whined again and she held him close, and Gabe thought, *Why not me? If you want comfort, why not me?*

It was a dumb thought. *Back away*, he told himself. *You've kissed her, do you want to take this further?*

Yes.

That was another dumb thought, but it was there and it wasn't going away.

Clothes. Practical stuff. Any minute she'd figure she was freezing and, as if the thought was relayed, she shuddered again.

'There's dry stuff in the locker below,' he said, and his voice came out gruffer than he intended. 'It might not be what you're used to...'

She rose. Wiped her wet hands on her tight wet jeans. Made a visible effort to pull herself together. 'Dry?'

'There's towels, overalls, sweaters, boots. We're used to wet. One size fits most. Or actually one size doesn't fit anyone—spares are huge; you roll 'em up, tuck 'em in, do what you can. Best I can do, I'm afraid.'

'The best you can do is awesome,' she whispered. 'I'm sorry I yelled.'

'You had a fright.'

'So did we all. And I'm still sorry I yelled. I never meant...I would never mean...'

She ran out of things to say. Instead, she reached for him, took his hands in hers, kissed him again, lightly on the lips, a feather-touch. And then she was gone, slipping below, leaving him with one sodden dog who was looking as confused as he felt.

CHAPTER EIGHT

THE trip home was made in near silence. Too much had happened. Too much was happening.

Nikki towelled Horse and cuddled him while Gabe stayed in the wheelhouse. He needed to stay in the wheelhouse. The fact that he wanted to be on the deck with them was irrelevant. More than irrelevant. There were things going on that needed careful thought.

When your foundations shifted, you didn't race to build again. You waited to see if your foundations shifted some more.

That was how he felt, he decided, as he headed back to harbour. As if the solid ground had been pulled from under him.

He didn't know where to take this. He didn't know…anything.

Horse, at least, had settled. He draped himself over Nikki, he whined occasionally but he'd stopped looking at the horizon.

By the time they reached port he was dry and starting to scratch.

Gabe steered the *Lady Nell* back into her berth. Crew members usually stepped onto the jetty, attached stays to bollards, helped.

Nikki didn't know what crew members were supposed to do. She stayed where she was, under Horse.

Gabe could manage. He'd taken the boat out by himself a thousand times. He'd taken his boat out with crew a lot more.

Taking it out, even with a crew, seemed lonely compared with what he'd had today.

Woman and dog.

Remember Lisbette, he told himself harshly. The one time he'd let himself believe, he'd come close to losing his livelihood.

He'd been lucky. Then it had just been Gabe who'd been affected. If it happened again…if he got into financial trouble now, the fishing industry of this town could well go under.

A man needed to keep his head.

Steer clear of women.

How could he do that now? Where were resolutions when you needed them?

He roped the last stay, tightened cleats, collected Nikki's wet gear from below.

Nikki struggled to rise from under Horse. He couldn't help himself. He gave her a hand and tugged her to her feet.

Mistake. She was too close.

His hand didn't release hers.

Horse scratched. Distraction. Good.

He managed to get his hand back.

'He's spent too much time in salt water,' he said, deciding he had to concentrate on the practical. 'All that sponging I did last night has been undone. He'll scratch himself sore with the salt. There's shampoo you can buy at the Co-op. Ask Marcia. She'll tell you. Tell her I sent you or she'll sell you the expensive stuff.'

'Thank you,' she said. 'Gabe…'

'Yes?' He turned away, tugged up the hatch, showing by his actions that he was moving on.

He was thinking he should go home and help her bathe the dog.

He had crays to deal with. A man had to be sensible.

Dog. Shampoo. Bath. His thoughts were no longer sensible in the least.

Nikki.

He had to give himself time to get his head in order.

Stay clear.

Nikki was a smart woman, he told himself harshly, and Horse was docile. She could bathe the dog.

Her bath was big enough. But the thoughts wouldn't be vanquished. Dog. Shampoo. Bath. He had a clear vision of them in her bathroom, in the vast old tub, soap everywhere…

Um…no.

'You were wonderful,' she said.

'And you weren't shark meat,' he retorted, not turning back. Determined on being sensible. 'Excellent.'

'It is excellent,' she said. 'For all sorts of reasons. Come on Horse, we're going home.'

And Nikki and Horse stepped from the boat onto the wharf without him even helping. They walked away.

He concentrated on the crays.

He didn't watch their going, but it took real effort.

Nikki and Horse walked slowly home around the headland, following the cliff path so they wouldn't necessarily see anyone. She had some pride, and the oversized overalls and huge fisherman's Guernsey weren't exactly elegant.

Nor was her dog.

'We match,' she told him. Horse was plodding wearily beside her. She should never have taken him on the boat. He should have slept today.

He should be sleeping now.

He looked desolate, big and ragged and defeated. It wasn't his health, she thought. It was his heart. He'd leaped into the water to follow what he thought was someone who loved him.

They were on the dirt track in the middle of bush-land leading back to the house. No one was around. She squatted and hugged him.

'It's okay,' she told him, burying her face in his salt-encrusted coat. 'You can move on. It's possible.'

Like she was moving on? By kissing Gabe instead of kissing Jonathan?

'I didn't actually do it to distract me from feeling bad about Jonathan,' she told Horse, who didn't understand at all. 'But it did distract me.'

It certainly had. She sat and hugged her dog, the sun shone on her face and she thought…she thought…

Life was full of possibilities. Exciting possibilities.

Possibilities that looked pretty much like Gabe Carver.

She'd thought she was alone, but she wasn't quite. A couple of elderly walkers strode round the bend and she had to shift so they could pass. They were stocky, sensible women with hiking poles, walking with intent.

They reached her and stopped.

Two days ago she might have cringed. Woman pulled from sea, dressed in fisherman's clothes, hugging a scraggy dog. This was pretty much as far from her life in Sydney as she could get.

'Are you all right?' one of the women asked, and she even managed a smile.

'My dog's a bit subdued,' she said. 'We're having a wee rest.'

'That's not one of Henrietta's dogs?' the woman demanded, staring down at Horse. 'I remember him. I saw the accident when the dogs escaped. This one just bolted. Terrified. And you'll be the lady living with Gabe Carver. I saw Hen at the post office this morning and she said you're keeping him. Oh, my dear...'

'I'm not looking after him very well,' Nikki admitted. The sun was warm on her face. Horse was settling. She was prepared to be expansive.

The world felt expansive, she decided. Plus the way the lady had said it... *You'll be the lady living with Gabe Carver.* It gave her a local identity, something she hadn't had until now. She wasn't sure why, but she liked it. Maybe it was sexist. Maybe it was stupid. Whatever, but she still liked it. 'Gabe took us out on his boat this morning and we fell in.'

'You fell in?'

'Gabe took you out on his boat?'

Both women looked at her, then looked back at each other. Stunned.

'I went to help with the cray-pots,' Nikki said, the odd happy feeling not fading. 'But we were worse than useless. We caught some crays. Then Horse dived in and it was all downhill from there.'

'Horse?'

'My dog.'

My dog. That sounded good, too. It sounded great. There were things happening inside her that felt delicious.

She hadn't planned on staying out today. She should be rushing home now to finish her engineering plans. But instead she was sitting in the middle of a walking trail discussing her very exciting morning with a couple of strangers.

Discussing Gabe?

'That's his sweater,' one lady said and Nikki glanced down at the oversized Guernsey and giggled. Being caught in Gabe's sweater felt good, too.

'He had spare clothes,' she said and grinned. 'I didn't pinch his.'

'Oh, my dear…'

'Where's Gabe now?' the first lady asked.

'Unloading his crays. I'm going home to bathe Horse. He's itchy.' She hesitated. 'Though I'm not sure how. I could use my bath but I don't trust the plumbing. And how would I lift him in?'

'Gabe might help,' the first lady ventured.

'Gabe?' the other said incredulously and they both made wry faces.

'Gabe might do it,' the lady explained as Nikki looked a question. 'But he'd do it at midnight when no one was looking. He's a very private person, our Gabe. He helps. But he helps when no one's looking.'

'That's not a lot of use to me,' Nikki said. Waiting

for Gabe to bathe Horse at midnight? Maybe not. 'Don't worry. I'll manage.' She had to. This was her dog. She needed to be independent.

But he was so big!

'I'll tell you what,' the first lady said. 'You take the doggy home and let him have a sleep. He looks exhausted. Maudie and I will finish our walk, we'll fetch the right shampoo for an itchy coat and we'll drive my truck around and help. I have a big plastic tub; I'll bring that. I'm Hilda, by the way, and you must be Nikki. While we bathe your dog you can tell us all about yourself.'

Nikki considered. She should bathe Horse herself. Or wait for Gabe?

The first might be impossible.

The second?

A girl had some pride. She'd kissed him. That didn't mean she depended on him.

She'd been dependent on a man for the last four years, she told herself. If she was to be independent, the time to start was now.

But Horse was enormous. Be sensible. She needed to accept help when it was offered.

If she was going to be a part of this community she might as well start now.

'Thank you,' she said. 'That would be lovely.'

She could be a little bit dependent, she decided. She just couldn't be dependent on Gabe.

* * *

A working bee was therefore following her home.

Horse headed for his trampoline, flopped and was asleep in seconds. Nikki showered, then tried to figure what to wear for dog bathing. Her one pair of jeans was sodden, everything else was classy and she didn't want to scare Maudie and Hilda with her city clothes. Finally she simply put Gabe's clothes back on. She felt ridiculous, but oooh, she was comfortable.

She stared at herself in the mirror. Fisherman Nikki.

Her hand reached automatically to the can of product designed to smooth her crazy curls. She flicked the power switch on her straightener—and then flicked it off.

She ran the hairdryer through her curls and they flew every which way. She looked at her reflection and she hardly recognised herself.

She grinned.

What next? She needed to stoke up for dog-washing.

She headed for the kitchen. Made herself a cheese sandwich. Considered. Made another. Sat on the doorstep in the sun and ate them. Thought about the sushi and black coffee she'd have eaten at her desk back in Sydney.

Hilda and Maudie were taking ages. While she waited, Horse slept.

She looked at the gap in the stone wall and it looked back at her.

It was Gabe's hole in the wall. Do not touch.

Find her own?

She had work to do. Air conditioning plans.

In Gabe's study, his books on dry stone walling...

Find your own.

She headed down to the pile of stones by the hole in the wall. Picked up stones, considered them, matched them, put them back on the pile. Gabe's hole in the fence remained just that.

Just practising. Just learning. Keeping an ear out for Gabe's truck so she could disappear fast.

There must be somewhere round here where she could get her own pile of stones.

Maybe there was someone to teach her.

Plans. Engineering. Her career.

The sun was too warm to think about plans.

She'd finish this set of plans, she told herself, and the next contracted job. But then...

She had enough money to be independent for quite a while. Her pay for the last few jobs had been enormous, and living in Jon's apartment had cost very little.

She'd been living Jon's life.

'This could be *my* life,' she said out loud.

Then she heard a 'Halloo' from along the road. Maudie and Hilda had arrived, bearing dog stuff.

'We're here to help,' Hilda called. 'I have the

world's biggest ice-bucket as a bath. We have shampoo and conditioner and scissors and brushes and
two hairdryers and six old towels. Do you think that
should do it?'

'I hope so,' Nikki said and grinned. She felt as
if she was stepping into a new life. Or maybe she'd
stepped into it the moment she'd met Horse.

Or the moment she'd hit Gabe over the head?

There were people in his front yard. Lots of people.
Seven? Eight? Ten?

They'd lit the barbecue.

When he'd asked Dorothy in the rental agency
about setting this place up, she'd included a barbecue on her list.

'Put in a barbecue where your tenant can cook
and see the sea. It'll almost double the rent.'

Up until now it hadn't been lit.

It was lit now. He climbed out of the truck and
the smell of sausages and onions hit him like a siren
song.

'Gabe!' It was Henrietta from the Animal Shelter, waving a bread-wrapped sausage. Henrietta's
son was on barbecue duty. He recognised Hilda and
Maudie, founding members of the town's stalwart
walking group, deep in conversation with Joe, his
own personal handyman.

Joe's springer spaniels were checking out Horse.
Horse was snoozing on his trampoline which had

obviously been brought outside so he could catch some late afternoon sun.

Nikki was deep in conversation with a lady older than Methuselah.

Aggie, Henrietta's mother. What the…?

'Nikki needed help bathing Horse,' Henrietta called, her voice filled with reproach. 'Where have you been?'

'I took a load of crays to Whale Cove.'

'Nikki needed help.'

'He's Nikki's dog,' he said shortly. *What was Aggie doing here?*

'It doesn't matter. We got on fine without you.' Nikki smiled and waved and he was hit by a blast of…difference.

She was still in his clothes. They were way too big for her. He'd thought until today that her hair was straight. Her hair was currently a riot. Curls everywhere.

She was sitting on the grass beside Horse. The springer spaniels were at her feet, nosing Horse, who was interested but he wasn't getting off his trampoline.

Someone had carried a chair outside for Aggie. She was about a hundred. Best guess. She'd been about a hundred ever since he could remember.

What was she doing here?

'Tell us what you think of Horse,' Henrietta demanded. 'Horse, show Uncle Gabe what you look like.'

Uncle Gabe? He had people in his backyard. He was starting to feel…

Horse stood up. It was a bit of a struggle but he managed it. His great tail wagged and something inside Gabe…

No. Don't go there. That ended with Jem.

He tried to look—dispassionately.

Horse had been worked on. Bathed. Combed. Anointed. The remnants of his coat were gleaming, knots cut or teased out, then brushed until it shone. He wobbled a little on his long legs but his crazy tail wagged, the feathering underneath waving wildly. He looked almost beautiful. He looked… almost happy.

He flopped back down on his belly. He gazed up at Gabe and his tail still waved.

So much for dispassionate. He was a sucker for dogs.

And after all, he told himself, this was Nikki's dog. Gabe could bend and scratch him behind the ears without committing himself to anyone. To anything.

But what was Aggie doing here? And all these people…

No one messed with his privacy.

Renting out part of his house had been a bad idea.

'You approve?' Nikki asked and he could tell she

was anxious. She was kneeling beside Horse. Because he'd stooped to pat Horse, he was close.

Really close.

'He looks great.'

'Doesn't he?' She beamed. 'I know it looks like we've done a lot to a dog who needs to rest, but he just lay in the sun and we worked on him slowly.'

'We?'

'Hilda and Maudie.'

'And Henrietta and Joe and…and Aggie?'

'They came later, didn't you, guys?' She beamed round at all of them. 'Hilda met Joe at the Co-op and told him what we were doing. She suggested a barbecue so Joe got it working. There were spiders. Big ones. Even Hilda and Maudie suggested we needed Joe. And look at Horse.'

He was looking at Horse. It was safer, he decided, to look at Horse rather than Nikki.

'What do you think?'

Horse had draped himself back over his trampoline, three quarters on but a quarter out, as if he'd like to join in but he still needed the security of his own place.

The trampoline Henrietta had supplied was plain canvas, what a sensible dog needed, but someone—someones by the look of the people around him—had decreed plain wasn't enough. A soft green velveteen throw had been added. Also a couple of pillows that looked as if they were down-filled, soft and squishy. Two stuffed toys, a rabbit and a giraffe.

There was a sausage resting by Horse's nose, and a new red water bowl.

Horse looked bemused. As if he didn't have a clue what was happening to his life.

Like Gabe.

These people were barbecuing in his backyard.

Or…Nikki's backyard.

He'd strung a couple of wires on fencing posts when he'd first let the place, delineating boundaries, but until now no one had needed delineation. No one had been in the backyard.

He should have planted a hedge. Fast growing.

He still could.

Nikki was smiling up at him, standing, offering him a sausage, glowing, and he thought yep, hedge. Or back away fast. But…

'Why is Aggie here?' he asked.

Maudie handed him a beer. Aggie passed him a bowl of pretzels.

'Aggie's teaching me to make stone walls,' Nikki said and he almost dropped both.

Maybe his face froze. How did you control your face? He didn't know what he was showing but, whatever it was, it made Nikki's smile slip.

'What is it?'

'What are you playing at?'

'Sorry?' She didn't have a clue what he was talking about. Or did she? She'd seen the books. She knew about his mother.

'I taught his mother to make stone fences,' Aggie said sedately from her chair. The little old lady was wrinkled and gnarled and unfussed, unmoving. Watching Gabe thoughtfully. Watching Nikki. 'Best student I ever had. Last, too. After her, no one. No one wants to spend their days piecing little bits of stone together. Why would they?' Her voice grew sad, distant. 'They're all falling down, my walls. The walls Gabe's mama helped me build. They're built to last for generations but people knock holes in them. They use the capping stones for wedging gates open, that sort of thing. They break 'em and don't know how to repair them. Can't believe you want to learn.'

'You don't want to learn,' Gabe said flatly.

'Why not?' Nikki demanded. 'Why don't I?'

The question hung. They'd all turned to listen now, every one of them caught by the flat anger in Gabe's voice. He couldn't help it. Anger was just... there.

'I don't want my wall finished,' he growled, knowing as he said it that it made no sense at all.

'I know that,' Nikki said. 'I even understand it. Sort of. But this is nothing to do with you, or your mum, or your wall. I'm sorry I borrowed your books without asking, but you have them back now and that's as far as my interference with you goes. I told

Henrietta I was bored with what I was doing, that I needed a break while I thought about what I wanted to do. I told her I'd been playing…' She hesitated and then decided to be truthful. 'I'd been playing with your stones. It feels good. I'd like to try it, as a hobby at least. I told Hen and she went to get Aggie, and Aggie says she'll teach me.'

'I don't want you to.'

The flat denial didn't even sound like him. The words were from some gut level he couldn't begin to understand. And, of course, Nikki couldn't understand either.

'It has nothing to do with you,' she retorted, sounding astounded. 'I'm your tenant, Gabe. If I go out in the morning and learn how to make stone walls instead of sitting inside drawing plans, how can that be interfering with you? Or don't you want anyone to learn stone walling ever again because of your mother?'

There was no answer to that. No answer at all. She was right; he was being stupid.

He'd seen stone wallers working since his mother died; of course he had. There were none working locally, but occasionally he'd see them by the roadside outside this area. He liked their quiet craft, was glad that stone walls were still being built.

It was just…Nikki. It was how she made him feel.

He should never have let her kiss him. He should never have kissed her.

He thought of Nikki, in the water where he knew sharks fed. Nikki, on the night she'd hit him, staring down at him with her eyes full of terror. Nikki, hugging this bedraggled, unloved dog, jumping into the water to save him, bringing this motley collection of people back to his house. To his home.

'I have things to do,' he said curtly, knowing he was being a bore, not knowing what to do about it. Setting his beer and plate aside.

Horse whined.

'You're going to cook your own dinner on your side of the wire?' Nikki demanded with a flash of anger.

He'd hurt her. He'd hurt them all.

But what Nikki did on her side of the fence was her business. He should have climbed straight out of the truck and gone inside, closing the door behind him. Instead…they were all looking at him. Judging him.

'Our Gabe's a loner,' Hen said placatingly to Nikki, as if she was explaining the behaviour of a difficult dog. 'This is his space.'

'He's renting it to me,' Nikki said dangerously. 'I pay for this side of the boundary wire. If he'd wanted me to stay inside with the door shut, he should have written a different tenancy agreement. Gabe, these people helped me this afternoon. They're my friends. They're Horse's friends. So we will keep on with our barbecue. As I'll continue with learning how to make stone walls. This isn't about you, Gabe. This is my back lawn—my barbecue. You can accept my invitation to join us, in which case you'll be pleasant and not treat us as intruders, or you can head inside and keep your own company. Your choice.'

His choice. He made it.

He turned, stepped over the dividing fence and went inside.

She was shaking. Of all the boorish, rude, arrogant…

'Don't mind him, dear,' Aggie said comfortably. 'His dad brought him up hard and a leopard can't change his spots. Till his dad died, any kid who came here risked being horse-whipped and Gabe too, for inviting them. There's ghosts in that man's head and, like it or not, you've brought 'em out. Now, are you going to eat that sausage or not? Dry stone walling's not for sissies. If you're starting tomorrow you need to get your strength up. Don't mind Gabe; he's a good man at heart, even if he never let us close. You just stay on your side of the fence and let him be.'

Midnight. She'd gone to sleep and dreamed of sharks. And Gabe.

Horse was snoring under her bed. He grunted in his sleep and suddenly she was wide awake, staring at the ceiling.

Thinking of sharks—and Gabe.

She put her hand down and Horse nuzzled her palm. She liked it. Something warm and solid in the night.

Go back to sleep.

The sharks were still there. And Gabe.

She padded out to the kitchen, made a pot of tea, hesitated, made a cheese sandwich.

Horse padded after her. She grinned and made two.

She thought about going back to bed. Went out on the veranda instead.

The stars were hanging low over the night sky. The moonlight was glinting over the ocean.

Horse whined and nuzzled her underarm. They ate sandwiches together and watched the distant sea.

Horse settled his great head under her arm, on her knee. He sighed a great dog sigh, and she agreed entirely.

Too hard. Everything.

Gabe?

She should still be thinking about Jonathan, she thought. Was she doomed to forget one appalling man, only to focus on another?

Then Horse stiffened, whined and pulled away. Her hand instinctively grabbed his collar but Horse was swivelling back towards the house. The door opened—the porch door leading to Gabe's side.

Gabe.

* * *

He could have guessed she'd be out here. He'd heard the wuffling and thought maybe she'd let Horse outside without her. He was worried about fences. How high could Horse jump?

She had him safe. The big dog was straining towards him but she had him by the collar and she wasn't letting go.

She was wearing pyjamas. Cute pyjamas. Ivory silk with pink embroidery.

Her hair was a mass of tumbled curls. She looked...

Like a man should back into the house and close the door.

'I'm out here,' she said. 'You should back into the house and close the door. Or make me another entrance so you don't need to see me.'

'Nikki...'

'I'm sorry about your mother,' she said before he could get a word in. 'I'm sorry she died and left you alone. And about your dad, who sounds like he was a bully and a pig. But you rented this place to me. If I'm going to feel like it's home, I can't spend my time figuring whether you're likely to come through the door so you can avoid me. And,' she said, taking a breath, obviously gearing up to say something that took courage, 'you were rude to my friends. You need to apologise. Joe's sausages and onions were great.'

'Joe's not your friend,' he snapped before he could think about it. 'He works for me.'

'The two are mutually exclusive?'

'I don't want you in my life.'

Why had he said that? He had no right. He had no need. It was harsh, hurtful, unnecessary. He saw her flinch, then stand and back away. To her door.

'Gabe, what you're saying…it's nonsense.' She was starting to shake. 'You've never asked me to be in your life. I've never suggested…'

'You don't have to,' he said explosively. 'You just are. You stand there, looking at me… You make me feel…'

'How do I make you feel?'

'I don't want it. I don't do relationships. I don't want to feel—anything.'

'Then don't.'

'You're saying you don't sense it, too? This thing between us?'

'If I am, I'm keeping it under control a whole lot more than you are,' she said bluntly. 'You think I'm about to launch myself at you and dig in my claws? Of all the insulting…'

'I didn't say that.' He raked his hair. 'It doesn't make sense. What I'm feeling.'

'It doesn't,' she said, and somehow she managed to sound calm. 'I'm not Lisbette, Gabe.'

'I know that.'

'And I'm not interested in another relationship,'

she added and she thought… Was that a lie? Because the way she felt…

She didn't understand the way she felt. Gabe was voicing his confusion. Hers…she'd managed to keep it internal. Anger was a great help.

But… *This thing between us…*

Gabe was right. It was there, tangible, real. It had to be ignored.

This big man was wounded, needy, wonderful. She wanted to reach out and touch him. Heal him. Heal herself in the process.

He didn't want it. She couldn't.

'You want me to find somewhere else to live?'

What was wrong with him? Was he nuts?

The town thought he was nuts.

No. They thought he was a loner.

There was a fine line between loner and nuts, he decided, and the way Nikki was looking at him… He'd just stepped over it.

'I'm sorry,' he said heavily. 'I'm behaving like an oaf.'

'You are.'

'There's no need to agree!' He wasn't making sense, even to himself.

'Yes, there is.' She sounded wary. But also…amazingly, she sounded amused. 'You kissed me, but so what? The way you're acting… Why? There's no need to think I'm planning weddings, kids, holes from your side of the house to my side, mortgages, puppies and old age homes with rockers side by side.'

'Old age homes?' he said faintly.

'That's how you're looking. Like a man faced with the whole domestic catastrophe. It was a barbecue. Eight people, including you, plus three dogs. On my side of the dividing line. You want to go out tomorrow and buy some twelve foot high screening?'

'I said I was sorry.'

'You still look like you expect me to jump you.'

'I don't.'

'It was just a kiss. I was scared. People do stupid things when they're scared. I won't go swimming with sharks again and I won't go out on your boat.'

'I won't ask you to.'

'Aren't you the gentleman?' She hauled open the door to her side of the house. 'I'm going back to bed. Do you have anything else to say? If so, say it now. I paid three months in advance. You want to give me notice to vacate? That'll be nine weeks where we need to coordinate using this porch so you won't have to look at me. And,' she said savagely, as if this was the final straw, 'I won't even demand that you fix the pipes.'

'The pipes?'

'They still make noises.'

'Talk to…'

Joe. I know. I have. Because there's no way I'd

ask my landlord to take a personal interest. There's no way he would.'

'There's no need…'

'There's not, is there? Tell me in the morning whether you want me to vacate. Meanwhile, I'm going to bed. I'm taking my dog with me. I'll lock my door after me and stay on my side of the wall… Oh, and Gabe…'

He was way out of line. He was being an oaf and there didn't seem to be a thing he could do about it. Even Horse was clinging to Nikki's side, as if he knew who his friend was.

'Yes?' He couldn't even find the words to apologise again. He was appalled at his own behaviour.

'I *am* learning to make stone walls,' she said. 'Aggie's teaching me, starting tomorrow. We're working on restoring a wall out the back of Black Mountain, so if the idea offends you you'd better steer clear.'

'I'll be at sea tomorrow.'

'Hooray,' she said. 'You can head for the horizon and never think about us again. Come on, Horse, it looks like our peace in the moonlight is over.'

She walked inside with as much dignity as she could muster. Horse sidled in with her.

She stood with her back to the door and she shook.

Horse was shaking, too.

She was scaring the baby.

With something between a sob and a laugh, she knelt and hugged the big dog. He licked her face.

Ugh. It was as close as a girl could come to having a shower. A warm shower.

The urge to sob subsided. She sank so she was sitting on the floor with Horse draped over her.

They both stopped shaking.

She'd managed to make her escape with dignity, but it had been a near thing.

'He's just a bore,' she told Horse. 'He's a guy who's been brought up with no manners. A woman-hating, dog-fearing hermit.'

His crew liked him. Joe liked him. The town made excuses for him and they wouldn't do that if he wasn't a good man at heart.

Was it just her?

Was he reacting that way because she'd kissed him?

'I can't take it back,' she told Horse. 'I don't even want to.'

Drat him—he had her thoroughly confused. And Nikki was a girl who didn't like being confused.

'I'm straightening my hair again tomorrow,' she told Horse, but he didn't seem impressed. She wasn't sure if she was either.

'But I *am* going to learn dry stone walling. It'll be a great job for a dog to come along and help. You want to do that?'

She got another lick for her pains. Grinned. Pushed herself to her feet and headed back to bed.

'Coming?'

Horse looked at her. Looked at the door. Whined

Was he wanting the beach? Or Gabe?

Gabe or beach?

'Neither,' she said, tugging Horse to her bedroom with her. 'If it's your low-life owner, get over it. your future's with me. And if it's Gabe…exactly the same.'

He felt about two inches high. Justifiably. What had she done to deserve the lambasting he'd given her?

She'd borrowed his books? She was trying to learn how to make a stone wall?

She'd twisted his heart.

There was the problem. Heart-twisting. It made him feel as if he was wide open, vulnerable to a woman. Vulnerable to Nikki.

He'd been nuts to ever rent the apartment out.

But if he'd met Nikki any other way he'd have felt the same, he thought. It wasn't that she was living next door. It wasn't that she was dragging him into her life. It was just that she was…Nikki.

A man'd be mad not to want her.

He wanted her.

It was a hunger so fierce it made him feel his world was no longer stable.

He'd get it stable again, he thought. Maybe he already had. Even if he was to let weakness prevail, after tonight he'd burned his bridges. The way she'd looked at him…

He deserved nothing less.

Maybe it was just as well.

The fleet would be in at dawn. He'd help sort the catch and he'd be out again. Deep sea fishing, he decided. Out for four or five days.

He could rotate the crews so he could be out for weeks.

Great.

Or not great.

Nikki was just through the door. He'd hurt her.

So knock and apologise?

He'd already done that. Not one of his finest moments.

He had to do something. He couldn't just leave.

That was exactly what he intended.

She heard his alarm through the wall. Five a.m.

Horse whined and hauled himself up beside her. Her bed was ridiculously small. What sort of masochistic streak had made her buy a single bed? No matter, she wasn't pushing her new pet off.

'Gabe's going fishing,' she told him. 'It's just as well. He's…unsettling.'

Unsettling or not, when she heard his truck disappear she felt…she felt…

Like she had when Jonathan left—but worse.

She hadn't needed Jonathan.

She didn't need Gabe.

Liar.

How can you need him? she demanded of herself. You don't know him.

But she did. It was like…meeting a part of her that had been missing.

They were alike, she thought. Hers had been a barren childhood. Gabe's had been worse but something in him resonated with her, touched her at a level she couldn't begin to explain.

Nonsense. Sentimental garbage.

But then she heard his truck return. Footsteps. A heavy thump on the porch. Her heart twisted.

Nonsense or not, if he knocked…

He didn't. Receding footsteps. The truck's engine restarting. He was gone again.

Horse headed for the door, barking, sounding excited. She hopped out of bed and opened the door with caution.

An ice tub was on her back step.

Crayfish, prawns, mud-crabs, oysters, mussels were arranged to perfection on a massive tub of ice. A bottle of champagne was wedged on the side.

She recognised the champagne label and gasped. Even Jonathan would have been impressed.

A note:

Apologies. I'm not used to being social. Make yourself at home. I don't even mind if you go onto my side of the fence. Take care of Horse. Give him an oyster or six.

The ice tub was lavish. She should be touched by such a gift. She should at least smile at his note.

Instead? Desolation.

Expensive food. Champagne. Things.

Jonathan used to give her gifts when he left her.

She wouldn't waste this. She'd share, and not just with Horse. She had friends now.

But she wouldn't share with Gabe. Gabe, who couldn't apologise in person.

Did she care?

'I'm a woman of independent means,' she said out loud to the world in general, but she didn't know what she meant.

Independence...

Horse nuzzled her leg.

She wasn't independent at all. Luckily, she had Horse, and he was a dog she could lean on.

'Want an oyster?' she asked. 'Because I don't.'

CHAPTER NINE

A GIRL had to have a passion. If it couldn't be Gabe—and it couldn't—then the next best thing was stone walling, and at least there her passion was uncomplicated.

Quite simply, walling felt as if a lost piece of her had been reinstated. Sitting on the edge of a paddock, dirty, sometimes damp—Aggie paused for rain but not for showers—watching her wall grow, stone by stone, Nikki felt as if she'd found her home.

Aggie was a fine teacher, happy with nothing less than perfection. Her walls were built to withstand livestock, age and weather. Knowing she had a teacher who could give her those skills was a source of satisfaction Nikki couldn't begin to explain.

Aggie was content as well. 'If you knew how much it hurts to see walls I've built be damaged and no longer be fit enough to fix 'em... If you really love this, girl, it'd be my pleasure to teach you. And don't fret about an income. Farmers love these walls. They get the stones out of their paddocks, they get walls that'll last for a hundred years and they look great. It's win win. They even get grants for repair—they're heritage, you know. We can charge almost what we want to fix 'em and build more. If you're serious…'

There was no doubting she was serious. She worked and worked, and every minute she loved it more. Horse lay beside her as she worked. Dog paradise. Two weeks into lessons a rabbit stuck its nose from behind the fence. She'd tied Horse to Aggie's chair—even though they weren't in sight of the sea, she was taking no chances. But, 'Let him off,' Aggie said as Horse nearly went crazy on the end of his lead.

'Really?'

'Really.'

So she did and Horse spent the afternoon chasing rabbits, more rabbits and more rabbits still. He never came close to catching one, but every time one escaped he zoomed back to her, almost as if he needed to tell her about it. His big body practically vibrated with exhilaration.

She took him home that night as filthy and as happy as she was. She had a rabbit-chasing dog. She wanted to tell Gabe.

Gabe wasn't home. Again.

She'd barely seen him. He came home only to replenish supplies and leave again. Solitude was his life since his father had died; since the woman called

Lisbette had screwed him for everything he had. She understood—but it still felt bad when she turned into the driveway and Gabe's truck wasn't there; when she flicked open the curtains before she went to bed and there was no light in his window.

She was being dumb. Needy. Adolescent, even. She shouldn't be twitching the curtain to see if he was at home. She shouldn't care.

She didn't.

What a lie.

He'd spent so long at sea he was starting to see fish in his dreams.

He loved his work. He took pride in his fleet, in the men and women who worked for him, in their skills and endurance. He also loved Banksia Bay. After Lisbette he'd left, swearing never to return, but he'd left his house, his boat, the two things he'd salvaged from Lisbette's financial raid. So maybe he'd never intended to let it go completely, and when the fleet was in trouble he'd been glad to come home.

The sea was the same.

But, in truth, the last few years had even seen him tire of the endless sea. As Jem had aged he'd spent more time on land, reading in front of the fire, taking the old dog for gentle walks around the cliffs, cooking. Settling.

When Jem had died he'd headed back to sea. It was the only place he knew how to…be.

A man knew where he was at sea. Especially if the work was hard.

So now he moved from crew to crew, ostensibly to spend time with each of his skippers, to work through problems with each of the boats, but in reality it was because when he was on board the crew worked harder, and he could work to match.

If he worked, then he slept. Mostly.

He couldn't stay at sea for ever.

How long until she grew tired of playing with stones and took herself back to Sydney?

How long before a man could put her out of his head?

She finished the tail ends of her contracted work—the last part of her life as an engineer. She needed to make one last trip to Sydney and that part of her life would be over. She could make it a day trip.

She didn't want to leave Horse with Henrietta. Even though Hen was lovely and her boarding kennels were great, Horse still shook when he saw her.

She'd like to leave him with Gabe.

Fat chance. Gabe was never at home.

'Leave him with me,' Aggie said diffidently. 'My cat won't like it but it's time he had a spot of excitement. And you needn't worry. The walls around my place would keep a herd of elephants in.'

So she left Horse with Aggie and drove to Sydney. She'd checked Jonathan wouldn't be in the office. She left her final work on his desk—and her letter of resignation.

She walked out feeling not one shred of regret.

She wanted to ring Gabe and tell him.

How dumb was that?

Instead, she headed to a specialist work-wear firm. She bought heavy duty overalls, leather gloves, sturdy boots, goggles and a bright yellow jacket so she could be seen if she was working by the roadside.

Bright yellow, like Gabe's sou'wester used to be before he wore it in.

Gabe.

Her thoughts shouldn't always turn to Gabe.

They just did.

There was nothing left to do in Sydney. She'd left at dawn, thinking she might need to spend time in the office, but her former colleagues were cool. She'd dumped more work on them. There was no suggestion of socialising. The work gear had taken all of half an hour to buy so she was back in Banksia Bay by three. At Aggie's, Horse greeted her with joy.

'He's been sitting by the door all day, pining for you,' Aggie said. 'I've been fearful to let him out. I had to let him chase the cat to cheer him up. Mind, that might be the last time I can take care of him— if you bring him back, my poor old cat might leave home for ever.'

Nikki grinned. She hugged her dog and loaded him back into her car, resolving to buy Aggie's cat some gourmet cat food. Thinking she wouldn't need to leave Horse again anyway. Who needed Sydney? What more could a woman want than what she had right now?

Gabe.

Stupid or not, she wanted Gabe.

And he was at home.

Aggie's normal working day was nine to five. It was barely four when Nikki turned into the drive and Gabe was on the veranda. She could tell by his face that he hadn't been expecting her.

Her heart…quivered?

This was nuts. She was behaving like a moon-struck adolescent. The tension between them was a construct that could and should be eliminated. Now.

'Hi,' she said, pretending cheeriness. Horse, however, didn't need to pretend. He headed up to the veranda, leaped to place his huge paws on Gabe's shoulders and Gabe only just managed not to fall.

Adolescent or not, she wouldn't mind putting her arms there either. Holding.

Stupid. She was a mature woman approaching her landlord. Her rude, hermit-of-a-landlord who wanted nothing to do with her. Or her dog.

He was hugging her dog.

She turned her back on the pair of them and

started hauling stuff from the car. Carrier bags labelled 'Grey's Industrial Work Gear'. Cool stuff.

She lugged her bags up the porch steps. Gabe—and Horse—stood aside to let her pass.

'Work gear?' Gabe queried, and she flashed him a suspicious look. The way he'd said it…

'Get over it,' she said. 'You don't have a monopoly on wearing overalls.'

'You've bought overalls?'

'Four pairs. Serious stuff.'

'Aggie's still teaching you, then?'

'I imagine you've heard. Five days a week. I went back to Sydney today to drop final plans off and to resign. Then I went and bought overalls.'

'You've resigned?'

She sighed. 'Yes.'

'You can't be serious.'

'What on earth does it have to do with you?' she demanded. 'Just because your mother made stone walls, is that a reason no one else can?'

'Only you.'

Only you. The two words hung. She didn't know what they meant, but she did know they were important.

'What is it about me,' she said at last, 'that makes you think I can't be a stone waller?' *That makes you think I'm threatening?*

'Nothing.'

Horse had sunk to all fours and was nosing

Nikki's packages. They were interesting. They were tools for her new life.

She was not going to let this man interfere with it.

Get it onto a normal plane, she told himself. Forget about...*this thing between us.* Move on.

'Come and see what we're doing,' she heard herself say, surprising herself by the dispassionate tone she managed. 'We're working behind Black Mountain on Eaglehawk Road. We'll be there tomorrow from about nine.'

'I'll be back at sea tomorrow.'

'Only if you want to be. You're the owner of the fleet. You can decide.'

'I can't make money unless I go to sea.'

'Maybe you have enough money,' she said gently. 'That's what I've decided. I've been doing a job that fills my head and my bank account, but not my heart. Horse and I are moving on.'

'I give you three months tops before you're bored.'

'How long did your mother build for?' she asked—and then regretted it. The look on his face...

He had demons, this man, and she didn't want to make them worse.

'You don't need to answer,' she said, softening. 'I had no right to ask. Don't come and see what Aggie and I are doing—I'm sure you're not interested and if it reminds you of things you'd rather forget then it's not worth the pain. Let me pass now, Gabe. I'll see you next time you're on shore.'

He stared at her for a long moment. His face was blank and still.

He wanted to say something, she thought, but he didn't know what. Or he didn't know how.

He was a big, silent man with demons. She wanted, quite suddenly, quite desperately, to hold him. Just hold him until the demons disappeared.

This wasn't an adolescent crush, she thought. There really was some intangible link…

'Gabe…'

'I'm holding you up,' he said and moved aside so there was no danger of her brushing against him. 'You have things to do.'

'Unpacking,' she managed, trying to sound cheerful. Trying to sound unconcerned. 'I've been shoe shopping. I have steel capped boots. They'll be eating their hearts out on the Paris catwalks.'

He smiled but only just, and the smile didn't reach his eyes. 'Sensible,' he said gruffly.

'That's me. Sensible.'

'Can you get your job back when you…?'

'I don't want my job back!' Enough of cheerful. Enough of sympathy. She practically yelled the words. Glared.

'Happy stone walling, then,' he said grimly.

'Thank you.'

There was nothing else to say. She walked straight

by him. Horse cast him a doubtful glance and then followed his new mistress home.

Why couldn't she get Gabe out of her head? Why was he messing with her equilibrium? Why?

He was damaged goods. He made no effort to be friendly. He didn't want anyone close.

She was forging her own life. She was making friends. She could live happily ever after.

She could buy her own little house, she decided, with a big backyard for Horse. Then she wouldn't have to see Gabe except in occasional passing, one resident of Banksia Bay to another.

She had enough money for a decent deposit. She could start searching straight away—before she annoyed Gabe so much he evicted her.

She should be proactive in her dealings with men.

In her dealings with Gabe.

That was sensible.

But there was a part of her that was refusing to be sensible. Even if Gabe didn't make her feel…like she did…she kind of liked living next door to him.

'It's safety. It's because he's the size of an oak,' she muttered to Horse, but she knew it was much, much more.

She stalked into the kitchen, put on the kettle, picked up one of her pretty china cups.

Looked at it with care.

'That's what Gabe thinks I am,' she told Horse.

'Tomorrow I'm buying mugs. Can you buy industrial strength mugs as well? And I'm changing into my new stone walling gear now.'

She'd invited him to see what she and Aggie were working on. Wanting to go was irrational, but he couldn't stop thinking of it.

It was as if there were chisels wedging themselves under the armour he'd spent thirty years building.

Why?

She was his tenant. She was learning to do dry stone walling with Aggie. Both of those things were unthreatening; neither should pierce his armour.

They did.

He had to get used to it. The new normality was that Nikki was his neighbour, his tenant, the local stone wall builder.

He would go and see one of her walls, he decided. He could behave rationally, it was simply that he hadn't until now.

The forecast for the next few days was for bad weather. He knew the crew would prefer to stay in—he'd been working them all too hard. The grass around the house needed mowing. He'd do that tomorrow—and then in the afternoon he'd casually drive around the back of Black Mountain and see where Aggie was working.

Both Aggie and Nikki.

* * *

The day was warm and blustery. 'We'll be in for a storm tonight,' Aggie said, settling down with her folding chair and her Thermos. The old lady was supremely content. Her body was failing her, she could no longer handle the stones, but she could watch Nikki with a gimlet eye, ordering Nikki's hands to do what Aggie's longed to.

In Aggie, Nikki had found a world-class stone waller, and a world-class teacher. She realised that as she worked, as Aggie's eyes found the perfect stone in seconds while Nikki would have searched an hour, as Aggie decreed a fit Nikki thought perfect was appalling— 'It'll blow a gale through the cracks; take it out and start again.'

The work was physically demanding but satisfying on a level Nikki had never guessed she needed. The farmer whose property they were working on came often to inspect, and his pride and pleasure added to hers.

'I never thought I'd get this fence fixed,' he told them. 'It's been here since my great-great-granddad's day. I've been filling the gaps with wire but now Aggie has a student… Lass, you'll have your life's work cut out for you.'

It felt great.

Horse agreed. When Nikki moved, so did he. He was becoming hers, Nikki thought with even more satisfaction.

This was her perfect life. Except for the small niggle of Gabe.

Who turned up mid-afternoon.

She was having trouble fitting a stone. Aggie assured her it'd fit; she just needed to rotate the stones above and behind. She was figuring whether she'd have to chip a bit off the stone—a process Aggie regarded with scorn as there was always the 'right' stone—when suddenly Horse was on his feet, wagging his shaggy tail and barking with delight.

'Look who the cat dragged in,' Aggie said, her voice full of pleasure as Gabe climbed from his truck.

He was wearing jeans and T-shirt, not as rough as usual. He'd shaved.

He still looked big and dark and dangerous.

He still made her heart flip.

'To what do we owe this honour?' Aggie demanded, and Nikki thought thank heaven for Aggie because there was no way she could think of anything sensible to say.

'I decided I'd come and see if she's as good as my mum,' Gabe said and smiled at her, and her heart did a backward somersault. *As good as my mum...* What sort of statement was that?

A statement without anger. A statement of a man accepting things as they were.

'She's got a long way to go but she's going to be better,' Aggie said roundly. 'Your mum had distractions. Husband. Baby. A working girl needs to focus.'

'So Nikki's focusing?'

'Yes, she is. Don't you distract her.'

'I wouldn't dream of it.' He hesitated while Nikki found another stone and tried to fit it. It was nowhere near the right size. Funny, maybe her mind was somewhere else.

'You coped with distractions,' Gabe told Aggie mildly. 'I seem to remember a husband, kids, a farm and a fishing boat. And world-class stone walling medals.'

'My Bert supported me,' Aggie growled. 'He was one in a million. He'd spend the night fishing, sleep for a couple of hours, then if I was on a rush job he'd come out and sort stones for me. They don't make 'em like Bert any more.'

'What did you do with the kids?' Nikki asked, fascinated.

'Playpens,' Aggie said. 'They don't hold with 'em any more, do they? But I had 'em corralled while I worked, then, as soon as they were big enough, they sorted stones. Can't figure why none of them wanted to stone wall for a career.'

'I can't imagine,' Nikki said faintly. She caught Gabe's eye and laughter met laughter.

He made her toes curl.

'Can I help?' he asked and there was a statement to take her breath away.

She didn't need to answer. Aggie was way before her.

'Sure you can,' she said, beaming. 'Nikki's got a way to go to get those muscles strong enough to set the base stones. There's a good twenty yards where they've been moved out of alignment. Some moron decided to drive cattle through here, can you believe that? They pushed a bulldozer through the lot of it. Twenty yards when two would have done. How fat's a cow? At least Frank wants it fixed now, so we just need you to dig along the line, flattening a trench and I'll tell you what stones to put in. Spade's in the back of my truck. What are you waiting for?'

The laughter was still there, Nikki thought. It was suppressed—there was no way Aggie would concede anything she said was funny—but it flashed between Nikki and Gabe and it warmed something she hadn't known was cold. It made her feel...

'If you stare at that stone for any longer it'll grow teeth and bite you,' Aggie snapped. 'We're wasting time. With Gabe to help us, I reckon we can get a couple of yards done by dusk. Get to work.'

'Yes, ma'am,' Nikki said and Gabe saluted and grinned and went to get the spade.

It felt weird.

It felt excellent.

Hard physical work—and it was hard, as hard as hauling in nets, as heaving crates of fish.

Digging along the trench. Setting the lines so he

could pack straight. Then heaving rock after rock into the trench, following Aggie's orders, moving, shifting, discarding, trying again, until he had the perfect line.

Normally an afternoon like this he'd be frustrated, stuck at home, itching to get to sea again.

He was having fun. Being bossed by one tyrannical old lady.

Listening to Nikki being bossed.

Watching Nikki take pleasure in her stones.

He remembered his mother. 'There's nothing like it, Gabe, when you find the perfect stone and it fits like it's meant to be there. When you know that's its place.'

She'd never locked him in a playpen or ordered him to help, but he had helped, and the pleasure of it returned to him now.

He'd never remembered his mother without pain, but this afternoon...watching Nikki...

His mother seemed to be there. And Jem.

Horse was lazily watching, and it seemed the ghost of Jem was with him as well. There was a peace here he hadn't known was missing.

The armour was peeling back.

He worked on. Little was said, but when Aggie got vocal, chastising them for fools, idiots, anyone could see that stone was way out of line, he flicked a glance at Nikki and their shared laughter grew.

And something else.

Something that had nothing to do with his mother. Or Jem. Or anyone or anything else.

It was something about the way Nikki knelt, intent, her crazy curls—how long since she'd abandoned that sophisticated straight cut?—flying in all directions. It was watching her sorting, fitting, rejecting, choosing another, listening to Aggie's criticism, sitting back, surveying what she'd done and finally, finally accepting that she'd found the right stone and the right place.

She'd give a tiny sigh of happiness as the stone slotted in and, as each stone fitted, she'd turn and hug Horse and tell him how clever he was for helping.

Horse wagged his tail, accepting praise with decorum.

Dog and woman looked totally, gloriously happy.

She was a city girl. A highly trained specialist engineer. This wasn't her world.

It looked as if it was her world.

He thought back to the woman he'd met the day she'd moved in. She'd worn a sophisticated outer skin. Now it seemed she'd shed it and she was who she truly wanted to be.

She was beautiful. Dirty, bedraggled, windblown, totally absorbed, she was the most beautiful woman he'd ever seen.

He turned a little and found Aggie was watching him. Bemused.

'A worthwhile project,' she said and grinned, and Gabe figured he'd never blushed in his life and he wasn't about to now.

'It'll be good when it's finished,' he said.

'She's beautiful now,' Aggie said and she wasn't looking at the wall. Her grin broadened but then a sudden gust of wind slapped around the slight shelter their partially made wall was giving them, and Aggie's hat sailed off her head, a woollen beanie. Gabe retrieved it, Aggie sighed, shoved it on her head and pushed herself out of her folding chair.

'That's it. The hat barometer says it's time to call it a day.' She shoved her chair into the back of her disreputable truck. 'I drove Nikki here, but you can take her home. Can you fit that dog in as well?'

'Sure,' Gabe said and glanced at Nikki—and the laughter was gone.

Replaced by uncertainty? Fear, even? Just because he'd agreed to drive her home?

He'd been an oaf.

He had a lot of ground to make up.

They drove in silence. He wasn't sure where to start, and maybe she thought the same. But it was up to him, he decided as he pulled up at his house. At *their* house.

'I need to apologise,' he said, and she twisted in her seat and looked at him. Horse was at her feet, his great head on her lap. She'd been stroking him. Her hand stilled.

'I thought you already had.'

'Not properly.' He hesitated. 'I've been a git,' he said at last. 'My dog died four months ago. It threw me. I know it's dumb to get emotional about a dog, but I didn't want to have another around the place.' He raked his hair. Tried to figure where to go from here. 'Horse is your first dog?'

'Yes,' she said, brisk and cool. 'And I hope he lives for ever. But the way you reacted to me… It's not all about Jem, is it?'

'No.' He shook his head, trying to figure it out. 'You remind me of my mother.' It was trite. It was barely true. There was so much more, but he couldn't begin to put it into words.

'That's so what every girl wants to hear,' she retorted but, amazingly, she grinned. 'Woohoo. But I'll take it as a compliment. After a day with Aggie, I'll take any compliment I can get.'

'You're serious enough to cope with Aggie's criticism?'

'I've never been more serious. If I can make a go of it…'

'You will.'

'I intend to try.' She reached for the door handle but Gabe reached over, caught her hand and held.

'I haven't finished apologising.'

'You've said you were a git. And you gave me

crayfish.' She looked down at his hand holding hers and she couldn't quite stop a tremor entering her voice. 'That'll do nicely. Plus you've dug my trench, which I would have had to do tomorrow. It would have taken me all day and it took you two hours. So apology accepted, thank you very much.'

'Can I cook you dinner?'

She stilled. Looked down at their linked hands. 'You don't want me on your side of the wall.'

'I might have changed my mind,' he said. No. That wasn't enough. He had to say it properly. 'I was nuts. I do want you on my side of the wall. There's nothing I'd like better than to cook you dinner.'

'Can I bring Horse?'

A woman and a dog on his side of the wall. In his sitting room.

Nikki and Horse.

Suddenly Jem was right by him, egging him on.

The measure of a life well lived is how many good dogs you can fit into it.

Did that go for love, too?

He'd never truly loved. He didn't know how.

He could try.

He stir-fried prawns, Thai style, with chilli, coriander, snap peas, lime juice. He served them over rice noodles that melted in her mouth.

They ate on the veranda looking over the sea.

208 NIKKI AND THE LONE WOLF

Looking out over the hole in the stone wall. Looking out at the world.

'Where did you learn to cook?' she asked. She'd eaten at some wonderful restaurants in her time. What she'd eaten tonight was right up there.

'I've cooked since my mum got sick. It's fun.'

Fun. The word hung between them.

Fun, she thought.

Fun wasn't a concept that sat easily with this man.

'Do you cook on the boat?'

'Life's too short for a bad meal,' he said simply. 'I'll take you to sea one night and cook you calamari straight from the line. There's nothing in the world to beat it.'

I'll take you to sea one night... It was a promise.

She felt as if she were standing on the edge of a precipice.

He brought out panacotta then, so creamy it was to die for, with brandied segments of mandarin and slivers of chocolate on the side.

'When did you do this?' she demanded.

'This morning. Before I came to find you. When I decided the fleet would stay in port, I had the whole day to kill.'

So he'd planned dinner, and then he'd come to find her.

She wasn't sure what was happening. All she knew was that Gabe's grim face had disappeared. He was shedding something. Opening himself.

Horse was between them, stretched under Gabe's chair. Gabe was rubbing his belly with his boot. Horse was practically purring.

Horse, too, had eaten prawns for dinner. Life was looking good from Horse's angle.

From Nikki's as well.

Every night she came home from work with aching muscles. Tonight she wasn't feeling an ache.

'Can I ask if you and Aggie can schedule in finishing my wall?' Gabe asked and the night stood still.

'Do you really want that?' she asked, breathless.

'I do.'

'Gabe…'

'Mmm.'

'You're not just doing it to be nice?'

'I'm not,' he said, and his tone was suddenly back to being grim. 'I'm doing it because I've lived with ghosts all my life. They've controlled what I do, and now I've decided it's time I was doing the controlling. The ghosts can come along if they want— and maybe they will—but they can watch what I do rather than dictate.' He rose. 'Come and tell me what needs doing.'

He held out his hand, imperious, and she looked at it for a moment, considering.

But there was nothing to consider. This was Gabe. Gabe, whose outside armour held a man she was… wanting to love?

The concept was frightening, but not as frightening as ignoring the hand, turning away from the need.

She laid her hand in his and let him tug her up. She came, a little too fast. Ended up a little too close.

He smiled and kissed the tip of her nose. It was a gesture of laughter and friendship, surely nothing more, but it brought back the memory of that first kiss.

Of her need.

She tugged back a little—but she didn't let go of his hand. He smiled ruefully.

'Slow,' he said. 'I have the sense to be slow. The way I'm feeling…'

There was enough in that statement to take her breath away all over again.

But she kept breathing. A girl had to do something as he led her off the veranda and down to the pile of stones and the gap in the fence. Breathing was all she could manage.

Horse followed. They stood on the dew-wet grass and gazed at the pile of stones. The moon was just starting to rise over the sea. The wind was from behind them. The long, low house provided them with shelter. The night was…perfect.

'Where do we start?' Gabe asked.

'Where your mother left off. Did your father never want it finished?'

'My father loved my mother in his fashion,' he

said simply. 'He didn't show it. She loved me and she loved her walls. After she died…he hated us both.'

'That's appalling.'

'Yes, but it's past time I made my peace.'

'By finishing the wall?'

'By more than that.' He hesitated. She could feel things breaking inside him, two sides warring. One side winning? The side she was starting to ache for.

'By letting go of my ghosts,' he said softly, his voice almost a whisper. Intimate and wonderful. 'By moving into a future where life isn't grim and harsh. By seeing what's in front of my eyes.'

And his eyes were all on her.

She thought about that for a bit, standing in silence, her hands in his. It felt momentous. But also… It felt simple.

As simple as falling in love?

That was what it felt like. Right now, she was giving her heart.

She thought of the convolutions of falling in love with Jonathan, the sophistry of his courtship, the elegant dinners, opera, amazing weekends in exotic places, horizon pools, butlers, champagne breakfasts.

The lies, deceit, heartache.

For years she'd thought she loved. And yet, here it was, hands linked, nothing more. Nothing to be said while something grew.

He'd made no promises. But this was a start, she thought. And if he was prepared to start…

Her heart wanted to leap into the breach, declare what she was feeling, move forward right now. But there was still wariness in his eyes, as if he expected things to implode.

He was hoping it wouldn't. Hope was wonderful.

She turned into him and tugged him to her. Wanting him close. Just…close.

Nothing more. She held him, her breasts against his chest, feeling her heartbeat merge to his.

The feeling grew. Something huge.

'I don't know how to do this,' Gabe said simply, holding her close. 'I've never learned to…let go.'

'You've been married.'

'Not married. Joined by a contract to someone I didn't know. And you?'

'I felt like I was. It was a lie.'

'Same with me. Nikki…'

'Mmm?' She tugged away a little, looked up at him in the moonlight. Saw trouble.

'I don't want to hurt you.'

'I don't think you can.'

'If I don't know that myself…' Hesitated. 'My dad… He did love my mother. He wanted all of her. I'm afraid…'

'That you're like your father?'

'Yes.'

'You're not,' she said simply. 'I know.'

The wind was rising, swirling around either end of the house, closing in again in the trees beyond. They had this one triangle of peace.

One fleeting moment.

She suddenly shivered, a premonition. He felt it, held her close, tugged her harder against him.

'There's so much I need to learn,' he said.

'Me, too. But if I can learn about stone walls, I can learn about you.'

She tilted her chin and pushed herself up on her toes. He caught her face in both hands and kissed her.

Wonderfully.

She felt loved.

That was what his kiss told her. She felt the heat, the aching need, the longing, the sheer want.

The tenderness and the passion, leashed, held under control but only just.

The smell of him…the taste…the feel…

Gabe.

The kiss lingered, stretched out, filled her. She was falling…falling…and it was so easy.

So easy to fall in love.

It was done. Just like that. If he wanted to take her…

No. Not right now. Indignant for lack of notice, Horse whimpered and pushed his great head between them. Gabe released her and Nikki thought…

was there a touch of relief in the way he put her aside?

He'd committed, but only so far. There was still reserve.

Ghosts.

'No further,' Gabe said and she could have wept with frustration but he was right. If he wasn't sure…

She was sure.

'Of course not,' she said with as much dignity as she could muster. 'I…I need to go to bed. I have stone walls to build in the morning. It's all very well for layabout fishermen, taking every tiny excuse of a wee bit of wind to stay in port…'

'We've a gale predicted by morning.'

'Pussycat,' she teased and stepped back.

Go slow.

She didn't want to go slow.

And suddenly the muscles she'd forgotten about… ached.

'You know what I want to do?' she asked.

'What?' He still sounded wary.

'Have a bath,' she said. 'I haven't been brave enough. My pipes gurgle.'

'Your pipes…'

'Joe tried to fix them,' she said with patience. 'He hit them with a spanner. But they still make the most horrific gurgle. You want to come and hear?'

And she saw him withdraw, right there.

Okay, it had been a ruse. She didn't want to go

inside and calmly close the door on him. Come inside and see my etchings? Come inside and listen to my pipes?

Corny.

Unwise.

'I don't think that's wise,' he said, and she shrivelled a bit. Felt…stupid.

She'd kissed him. He'd kissed her back and it was wonderful, but the next step was up to him. His face said it.

This relationship would be on his terms.

Like her relationship with Jonathan. He called the tune.

She felt…a little bit ill.

'Sorry,' she managed. 'That was dumb.'

'Nikki…'

'No, you're right, standing in my bathroom listening to pipes there's every chance I could jump you. That'd be dreadful.'

'I didn't mean…'

'Of course you didn't,' she managed but she thought, bleakly, Gabe had his demons, but so did she. Standing back and waiting for him to decide…

Like she'd stood back and let Jonathan decide for years.

Pushing would get her nowhere. Do damage. Crush a bud that'd had no chance to unfurl.

The problem was that her bud had unfurled and

was wide open. She wanted this man in her arms. In her heart.

In her bed?

He'd just said no.

He'd said no to her pipes. Not to bed.

They both knew it was more.

'I can manage without a bath,' she said with as much dignity as she could muster.

'I'll check them in the morning.'

'That's big of you.'

'Nikki…'

'No, that was uncalled for. I'm sorry.' She lifted her hand and ran her fingers down his jaw, a feather-touch. 'I didn't mean to snap. You're being wise for both of us, and that's good. Tomorrow you can call the plumber. Not Joe but not you. You can come to my bathroom when you're ready but not before.'

There was still doubt. She saw it in his eyes.

He wanted her—she could see it, she could feel it, she could almost touch it. But he was…afraid?

'You're not like your father,' she said as evenly as she could. 'But I'm not Lisbette, either.'

'I know that.'

'You don't,' she said. 'Otherwise you'd check my pipes for me, right here, right now. Trust me, Gabe.'

'I do.'

'No, you don't. And whether you can learn… You can't open yourself a little and protect the rest. That's what Jonathan did. That's what I'm used to and I've moved on. I think…I think I love you, Gabe, but I'm not going to love a man who spends his life protecting his boundaries.'

She stepped back. Hoping he'd stop her.

He didn't and she felt sick.

Feeling bad was dumb. She should give him space.

She had to give him space.

Like she'd given space to Jonathan?

'Goodnight, Gabe,' she said as firmly as she could. 'Thank you for a wonderful dinner. Horse and I loved it. See you…see you tomorrow. Come on, Horse, bed.'

Why hadn't he taken the next logical step? No, the next instinctive step. The step every part of him except one tiny last shred of pathetic armour was screaming at him to take.

He was every kind of fool.

He'd wanted to pick her up and take her to his bed. As simple as that.

She'd have come. She'd yielded, every sweet part of her pressed against him, wanting him as much as he wanted her. But that scrap of residual armour was screaming that it was way too fast.

He was a loner. A man didn't give away a lifestyle in a heartbeat.

He headed out to the edge of the garden, staring

into the dark where the sea was starting to rise in the wind. He was staring into an abyss.

He remembered how he'd felt when his mother died. When he'd realised why Lisbette had married him. When Jem had ceased breathing.

How many times could a man expose himself to that sort of pain?

He wouldn't be exposing himself. This was Nikki he was wanting. Nikki he was falling in love with?

He'd been a loner for most of his life. Why stop now?

Because of Nikki.

But to let that sort of hurt in...

He could be sensible. One step at a time, he told himself. Take it as it comes, don't rush it, leave it so you can back out any time you want.

He had backed out. He'd refused to enter her house, to check her pipes, to do something so simple.

But he knew if he'd walked into her side of the house he'd have stayed there.

In her crazy bed?

A woman like Nikki needed a king-sized bed.

He needed a woman like Nikki.

Not tonight.

Yes, tonight.

No.

She'd walked away and closed her door. She was giving him space and he appreciated it.

He didn't. A man was a fool.

She was probably already running the bath. The thought of her…

He closed his eyes. He was falling…

Step away from the edge.

Tomorrow, he thought. Tomorrow.

How could he learn to trust—to shed that last vestige of protection from pain and gather her against his heart?

If he was wrong… If he hurt her… If they self destructed as his parents had…

It was one step forward and he didn't have the courage to take it.

'I don't want another Jonathan,' she told Horse, sinking onto the hall floor to give him a hug. 'Oh, but it's hard. How to make him trust me?'

If he didn't trust her there was nothing she could do.

Trust. It was throwing your heart into the ring. He worried that he was like his father. She'd told him he wasn't. She was sure of it.

Because she trusted him.

Maybe she was a fool. Maybe she was heading down the Jonathan path all over again.

Her whole body felt as if it was sensitised, every nerve tingling.

She knew what she wanted.

Not happening.

What to do?

She glared at the wall dividing her place from his. He was so close—and so far.

'Toerag,' she muttered but she didn't believe it.

But why couldn't he trust her? It hurt.

She felt exposed and vulnerable and a tiny bit stupid.

Okay, a lot stupid.

What to do? Go calmly to bed? Look forward to a nice polite good morning in the porch tomorrow?

Great.

She wanted, quite suddenly, to throw something. Hard.

How immature was that?

'Forget the pipes,' she told Horse. 'I'm having a bath. It's the only thing I can think of. A nice hot soak and see if I can get my body to behave.'

And her mind.

Bath. Instead of Gabe.

What a substitute.

'No matter,' she told Horse and climbed resolutely to her feet and marched into the bathroom.

Don't think of Gabe.

The bath ran beautifully, despite the gurgle. See, who needed a man?

And then…it didn't run beautifully at all.

He walked slowly back to the house, hands thrust in his pockets, deep in his thoughts. Glanced up at the house…

Nikki burst out of her door with Horse behind her and headed across the porch to his door. She thumped on his door as if she wanted to break it down.

She was wet to the skin. Soaking.

She was wearing a dripping bathrobe. She was carrying her purse.

She was carrying her car keys.

Horse was wet as well.

'What the…? What's happened?'

She swivelled and faced the darkness, trying to see him. Her glare made him take a step back.

'Ask Joe,' she snapped as she focused. *Snapped?* Maybe that was the wrong word. Yelled might be a better description. 'Don't you ever come onto my side of the house,' she mimicked. 'Because I might jump you. Instead, you send Joe and he comes and thumps my pipes with his spanner. Sooo useful. Not!'

'Nikki…'

But she'd barely got started. 'I ran a bath,' she said, spitting fire. 'It ran beautifully, even if it did make weird noises. So I hopped in and tried to relax even though I was smouldering. Smouldering, Gabe, and why would I be smouldering? Because someone round here doesn't trust me enough to check my pipes. And the water wasn't hot enough so I wiggled the tap with my big toe and suddenly the whole wall burst. I'm guessing the pipe behind the wall disintegrated.'

'Uh-oh,' he said. He couldn't think of anything more…wise.

'Uh-oh is right,' she snapped and he decided saying anything at all had been stupid. Really stupid. 'Or maybe you can think of something worse to say. I surely can. Because there's water shooting out all over the bathroom, but that's not all. The bath backs onto my bedroom and that wall burst, too. So my bed's soaked. And my wardrobe, and my dresser. Everything. So I've rung Aggie and I'm going there. You'll have to care for Horse tonight. Aggie's cat doesn't like him. Take his keep out of the amount I intend to sue you for. So it's over to you, landlord. Walk over my threshold and do something about it or phone Joe. Tell him to bring a bigger spanner, and my nine weeks' notice starts now.'

'Nikki, come in and we'll dry you,' he said, struggling not to laugh. She was a flaming virago, soaked to the skin.

But she wasn't seeing the humour.

'You'll dry me?' she demanded, barely getting the words out. 'What, with towels? Close? How do you know I won't jump you? You don't even trust me enough to check my pipes. What would happen with a naked woman and a towel? Get out of my way, Gabe Carver. I'm going to Aggie's. All by myself.'

* * *

He needed to gather her up, carry her soggy person into his side of the house, take charge. But he was… gobsmacked.

She stalked across the yard and flung the gate open, all flaming temper and outraged beauty. He was stunned to immobility.

By his side, Horse whimpered and Gabe agreed. He needed to fight the desire to laugh. He needed to…

But she was already in her car, moving fast.

Maybe she'd sensed the laughter.

'Nikki…' he yelled but it was too late.

Her car wheels spun on the gravel. She turned out of the gate and disappeared into the night.

And Horse lunged after her.

'Horse!'

He was too late there as well.

Nikki was gone and Horse had followed.

CHAPTER TEN

ANYONE but Aggie might have been surprised. Aggie, however, had a husband who'd fished and her sons still did. Wet didn't shock her, and when she opened the door to a dripping, seething Nikki she merely stepped aside and said, 'Bathroom's that-a-way—use the yellow towel. Yell at Gabe in the morning—get dry first.'

'How did you know it was Gabe's fault?'

'Has to be someone's,' Aggie said. 'You're looking hopping-mad. Gabe's closest. Male. Why look further? You want pyjamas, or something to sit up in and seethe a while longer?' Then the phone rang and Nikki was left to dry herself while Aggie went to answer it.

A minute later Aggie was back and an armload of clothes was handed round the bathroom door. Oversized trousers, a fisherman's sweater, thick socks, boots.

And Aggie's voice had changed. 'They're too big, but it don't matter. Get dressed fast.'

'Why?'

'Word is Horse chased after you. The road to Gabe's place hits the cove at the bottom of the hill, then rounds the bend. Horse didn't reach there before you disappeared so he must've figured you went the way of the last scumbag who owned him. He's headed out to sea. Phil Hamer noticed your car turn into here. You know you can't do anything round here without being noticed—he was on his way home from stocking the supermarket and wondered about me getting visitors late at night. Then he met Gabe further on, heading for the cove. He stopped to help but there was nothing he could do. Horse's already out past the breakers. Gabe's headed for the harbour to get the boat. Phil figured you'd want to know. If you head straight for the jetty at the entrance you might catch him. Otherwise, he'll be heading out alone. Filthy weather—he'll need all the help he can get. You're wasting time, girl. I'd come with you but I'd only hold you back. Go.'

He'd run, but Horse was on a mission and wasn't to be stopped. By the time Gabe reached the cove Horse was already in the surf.

He yelled, desperate. 'Horse!' No response. Of course not. Horse wanted Nikki.

'She's in the car, not out to sea,' he yelled and that was dumb as well because Horse wasn't listening. He'd seen Nikki disappear and he knew where people who disappeared went. He gave one long, low, despairing howl and swam for the horizon.

Gabe swore and swore again. Headed into the surf after him. Hoping he'd be washed in.

Maybe he would. Maybe he'd have the sense to realise he couldn't swim against the current—but the undertow was fierce. Gabe stood chest-deep in water, fighting the undertow, hoping the dog would turn.

Nothing.

The tide was going out. It'd be impossible to fight.

There was no sense trying to swim after him. Gabe knew he didn't have the strength to fight that sea.

He stood thigh-deep as the waves battered him, as he forced himself to think.

Outgoing tide. Northbound current. Big sea.

What hope of finding him?

Zero.

He felt sick to the stomach.

He was vaguely aware of Phil Hamer, the fussy little supermarket manager, uttering sounds of distress at the water's edge. Trying to give comfort.

There was no comfort to be had if he lost Horse.

He waited for as long as he dared, hoping against hope Horse could fight his way back. But even if he'd wanted to return… Once he was out the back of the surf the current would take him further.

He'd take the boat out. Try to find him.

He was a stray.

He was Nikki's dog.

He was Horse. He had to try.

But on a night like this... To take the boat out alone... It would be worse than useless.

He couldn't ask for help. To ask his crew to put to sea in the face of an oncoming storm for a stray dog...

'What can I do?' Phil bleated, immeasurably distressed.

'Nothing, mate,' he said bleakly. 'I'll head out and do what I can, but I need a miracle.'

She left the lights on in her car, shining straight out over the entrance. She stood out on the jetty at the harbour entrance, putting herself deliberately in the path of her car light, so whoever was in a boat heading out to sea could see her.

So Gabe could see her.

The wind was fierce and there was no moon. Water was washing up over the ancient timbers.

For an awful moment she thought she'd missed him. She stood in the rising wind on the tiny jetty and felt sick.

But then the *Lady Nell* emerged from the darkness and she started yelling. 'Gabe! Gabe!'

He couldn't miss her. Hysterical woman screaming at harbour mouth. Waving as if she were drowning.

He didn't veer in.

'Gabe!' She put everything she possessed into that scream and the boat turned. Came alongside.

'It's rough. You can't…' he yelled but he'd come close enough for her to jump and she jumped.

Possibly a distance an Olympian would be proud of.

She staggered, grabbed the handrail, lurched sideways.

But Gabe had her before she could fall, grabbing her, hauling her roughly against him and half dragging her back into the wheelhouse.

'What the…? You could have been killed. Of all the stupid…'

'Why didn't you come closer?'

'You weren't meant to jump. You weren't meant to be here. There's a storm coming.'

'You were going out without me? *To find my dog?*' Hysterical didn't cut it. She was screaming.

'I lost him.'

'He's my dog.'

'It's dangerous.'

'He's my dog!' She couldn't get any louder if she tried. But with that last yell… The adrenalin of dressing, driving way too fast to reach the entrance, thinking she'd missed him, jumping. Knowing she'd lost Horse… Something gave.

She folded and he caught her and held her hard against him.

She let herself crumple against him, taking mute

comfort in the size of him, the strength. The boat was heading out to sea. He wasn't taking her back.

'I can't let you risk…' he muttered.

She thought about that. Got incensed. Anger helped. She hauled back and thumped him hard on the chest. Started yelling again. 'What gives you the right to say who risks?'

'I lost…'

'You didn't. Horse lost himself. He's a crazy mutt who hasn't figured out for himself where his heart is. It's my fault. I shouldn't have left him. I shouldn't have lost my temper.' She thumped him again and it was like striking oak. 'So don't you dare say we can't share. We're finding him together.'

He folded her against him again, her thumps totally useless.

'We won't find him,' he said. Facing facts. Bleak as death.

'We can try. But we do this together.'

'It'd be better if you let me do it alone.'

'Better for who? Are you out of your mind? We love him to bits. We both love him and we both do this. Both or no one.'

Aggie watched Nikki leave and turned to the phone. No one could expect an old lady to calmly go back to bed when Horse was at risk.

Banksia Bay was a tight-knit community. Gabe

employed half the fishing fleet, and their families
and friends encompassed the town.

The dog community was big, too.

All she had to do was rally the troops.

She rang Henrietta first. 'Ring round, let people
know. Skippers of the other boats. Crews.' She hung
up as she heard Hen yelling at her son to get off the
Internet, to come and help.

Then she rang Raff. The local cop and Gabe were
mates. She had Raff onside in a heartbeat.

'I'll ring Whale Cove,' Raff said curtly. 'Harry
at North Coast Flight Aid owes me a favour or six.
If the chopper's free...'

But... 'It's a filthy night. Raff, this is for a dog,'
Aggie faltered, thinking she should just remind him.

'This is for *Gabe's* dog,' Raff said. 'This town's
been wanting to help Gabe for years and he doesn't
let 'em close. You think we'll miss a chance now?'

'It's Nikki's dog.'

'Same thing,' Raff said curtly. 'He mightn't think
so but the rest of us do.'

He knew the currents. Gabe knew the vague direction where Horse might be swept, but in the darkness in a storm-tossed sea...

The thing was hopeless.

He had to try.

He had, he thought, two hours maximum before
the storm closed in and he had to take Nikki home.

He hated that she was out here. He hated having to share this risk.

To risk Nikki…

She was out on the deck, watching desperately as his floodlights lit the sea.

His heart twisted in pain for her. And for him.

Horse was out here somewhere because he thought Nikki had headed to the sea. Three weeks of Nikki, and Horse knew where his heart lay.

Whereas he…

Tonight he'd backed off. He'd sent her to her side of the house alone. Then, when she'd appeared at her door, a drowned rat, a flaming virago, he'd stood like a great idiot while she yelled and handed over her dog and headed away.

Away from him.

He wanted to hold her, right now, desperately, but he had to stay in the wheelhouse and she had to search.

They needed more eyes.

Call for help?

Sure. Call the town, say, *Come out guys, risk the storm sweeping in early, to save a dog.*

This was his pain.

No. It was Nikki's pain. Shared.

This was what he didn't want to happen. This awfulness. Grief was to be faced alone. To make others share it was appalling. Worse than suffering it yourself.

He watched Nikki's rigid frame at the rail and he felt ill.

Her eyes didn't leave the sea. He was making parallel runs from behind the breakers to out where Horse could conceivably be swept.

So much sea.

Hopeless.

But then…

A helicopter came, sweeping in fast and low from the south. Searchlights flooded the ocean.

The radio. Raff…

'Gabe, that's Harry up there. Signal him that he's focused on the right boat. He'll pick up your frequency from this conversation.'

Harry—North Coast Flight Aid. What the…?

He signalled upward and Harry banked the chopper, heading into the cliff. Starting parallel runs of his own.

There'd be a crew in the chopper. More eyes.

'There's more boats coming out,' Nikki yelled, her voice cracking, and Gabe turned to glance at the harbour entrance.

This wasn't one or two boats. It was a flotilla, heading out into the storm.

What did they think they were doing? It was only just safe now. In another hour or two…

'We're thinking we have a two-hour window,' Raff yelled through the radio. 'Keith's back at base working out currents, search paths. He's allocating runs. You're furthest out, you do the north most run. Straight from where you are now into the back of the breakers and back again. You've only got one pair of eyes, so Nikki does the north lookout. *Mary Lou*'s got you covered; Tom has four aboard so he'll search your south side and his north, then the next boat takes over where his limit is. The chopper goes closer to the reef. Any questions?'

'I can't ask...'

'Who said anything about asking?' Raff snapped. 'Let's find this dog and get home.'

They were one of a pack.

Searchlights were playing over the water. Boats were everywhere—the flotilla was making parallel runs, heading into the cliffs, as close as they dared, then along, then out to the maximum distance the current could take a dog.

The helicopter was above, sweeping as well, so the whole surface of the sea was lit. They needed the moon, but with the approaching storm they had nothing.

They needed luck.

Nikki hadn't moved since they'd left the harbour. She'd hardly registered the approaching armada. She watched and watched.

Maybe she prayed as well. Gabe hadn't prayed since he was a kid. He prayed now.

One dog in a huge sea.

He might well already be drowned. He'd been near death three weeks ago. Three weeks wasn't enough to get his strength back.

He watched the sea and in between he watched Nikki.

What had he been thinking?

He'd tried to keep his distance.

He glanced around at the flotilla who'd set out in filthy weather to save one dog.

No one was keeping their distance this night.

And with that knowledge...something was breaking within him. The armour he'd built with such care...

He'd told himself he needed no one. He depended on no one.

Not true. It had been an illusion. It had taken one crazy dog and one loving woman to make him see the truth.

Plus an army of Banksia Bay dog-searchers.

Where was his illusion now? Gabe Carver, who walked alone, had ceased to exist.

For Gabe Carver was breaking his heart for a dog, breaking his heart for a woman, and there wasn't a thing he could do about it.

And the town, his crew, his friends... They were breaking their hearts for him.

A tiny flotilla in an approaching storm, searching the sea for one stray dog.

Where was the use of armour here? He tossed it aside and he knew it was gone for ever.

Horse.

Nikki.

The people surrounding him.

His heart was wide open.

Please…

There was no fast find here.

Back and forth. Back and forth.

Twelve-thirty. One.

The wind was rising, the sea steadily growing. Soon the helicopter would have to call it quits, and also the smaller boats.

Back and forth…

The chopper was making parallel runs ahead of the fleet, moving further out, making sure of the boundaries.

Slow, methodical sweeps.

Then, suddenly, as one of the smallest boats notified Gabe reluctantly that it was time to turn back, the helicopter banked and turned and hovered.

The down-draught flattened the sea close to the cliff.

The boats hadn't gone so far in. It was too close to the cliffs, too shallow, dangerous.

The chopper was hovering over a reef—Satan's Lookout. A shard of granite reached from the sea, further out than the bulk of the reef. A trap for un-wary shipping.

The radio crackled to life. Harry from the chop-per, yelling into his headset. 'He's down there. We can see him. He's clinging to the lee side of the reef. If it was a person we'd drop a harness but there's no way we can pick up a dog of that size. I'm not sure even you guys can get him off there.'

The good news? Horse was alive.

But Horse didn't do things in halves, Gabe thought. Swimming with sharks. Satan's Lookout. How many lives did one dog have?

Nikki was beside him, clinging. She must have seen his face change as he listened to Harry. 'What's happening?' she asked and if her face lost any more colour she'd disappear entirely. She was probably seasick, Gabe thought, and she hugged her stomach and he knew he was right.

What to do? Rough seas and shallow water. There was no way they could take the big boats close. They'd have to take a lifeboat.

But to steer close to the rock and lift Horse… They'd need two people to pull it off, Gabe thought, feeling sick himself. Usually he had Frank and Hat-tie as crew, both experienced. Tonight he had Nikki.

Nikki would never be competent enough to cope in the life-raft. Could he leave her at the wheel? Could he do it on his own?

No.

But to ask it of others…

The radio crackled into life again. 'Boss?' It was Bert, skipper of the *Mariette*. 'We're all lowering lifeboats. Mick and Mike'll go in ours. Sara and Paula are doing the same from *Bertha*, and Tom and Angie are coming off *Mary Lou*. That's three boats to look after each other. *Mary Lou*'s lifeboat's the most solid, so Angie and Tom'll try and get him off. There's backup to pick up the pieces if needed, and we'll use harnesses and link to each other. This dog doesn't bite, does he?'

'No, but…' His crew had obviously talked on another frequency. This was being taken out of his hands. What he couldn't ask was being offered.

'So he's a pussycat?' Bert demanded.

'A great hulking, sodden pussycat.' But his mind was racing. For others to risk their lives to save his dog… Nikki's dog… 'But I can't ask…'

'You're not asking, we're telling,' Bert said and there was even a note of humour in his voice. 'Takes a bit of getting used to, don't it? Accepting help. You just keep your nose into the wind and keep our Nikki from jumping over the side. We'll get her dog back to her in a trice. Or maybe in more than a trice but we'll get him back. Right, guys.' He was linked to the communal radio—obviously they'd changed frequency to hatch their plan but they were back on common frequency now. 'Let's go fish ourselves a dog.'

So Gabe was forced to wait, to stay idle, to depend on others, while men and women put themselves in danger over a dog he'd been stupid enough to let go.

He should have crew with him so he could do this himself. He should at least help. But there was no way he could ask Nikki, a seasick landlubber, to take over the *Lady Nell*. She had no skills.

But she did have skills, he conceded as he watched the lifeboats be launched. Different skills.

Changing direction and following her dream? Turning her back on her past?

Giving her heart?

She'd gone back to the rail. She was sick and cold and frightened.

He wanted to hold her.

He had to stay at the wheel. This sea was rough and getting rougher. It took experience and skill to keep the *Lady Nell* steady.

He had to depend on others.

He needed others.

He needed Nikki.

His armour was gone. He was no longer bothering to cling to remnants, no longer thinking about what he still needed to protect.

There was nothing to protect. What he needed was outside the armour.

Nikki. Horse. And these people—his crew, his town.

He felt terrified. Totally exposed. If one of those boats capsized…

They didn't.

There were three small boats with three magnificent seamen in charge. The chopper stayed overhead, flattening the water, lighting the scene like day. They all wore lifelines. If someone fell in, Harry would have someone down with a harness in seconds.

The biggest fear was right at the rock.

Horse was clinging to the lee side—sensible dog. But still, for a boat to get in there…

Angie was in the bow of the biggest lifeboat. Like him, Angie was born of a fisher-family. She was older and more experienced than he was, but she had three teenagers at home. What was she thinking?

She was going whether he permitted it or not. He was no longer in charge.

The focus of the community was saving a dog.

Please… It was a muddle of a prayer.

He should be where Angie was.

He had to stay at the wheel. He had to depend on others.

They were at the rock, Angie and Tom. Angie

was wearing a headset. Harry was watching the sea from above, giving her instructions. Watching the sea from on high.

Nikki was clinging to the rail, watching every move as if she could guide them by sight.

He wanted to hold Nikki.

His job was to hold the wheel and wait. And to depend on others.

And feel his foundations shift under him. He'd never felt such fear.

Depending on others.

They were twenty feet out from where Horse clung now. They were watching, waiting, waiting.

A lull. *Go.*

Did he yell it? His ears rang, maybe every skipper had yelled it in unison over the radio.

They were already there, surging into the rock. Angie stood to reach…

Horse had to let go.

'Let go of the bloody rock.' It was Angie, yelling into the radio headset like she boomed to the other boats over the water. It was a voice to wake the dead, to shock the unshockable, to make Horse release his grip.

And Angie had Horse around the midriff, dragging him back.

They were in the boat but they were still in danger. The next wave…

Tom had the tiller, the boat swung, hit the wave head on, rode through it—and they were safe.

The lifeboat headed for the *Lady Nell* rather than back to the *Mary Lou*. They figured Horse needed Nikki.

Still Gabe couldn't help. It nearly killed him, but he had to hold the *Lady Nell* steady so there was a modicum of shelter on the side they were boarding.

They made two runs before they got a patch of clear water. Angie heaved the big dog up as Nikki reached down.

Then Horse, almost flaccid until now, looked up and saw Nikki. His great paws found purchase on the side and Angie no longer had to heave. Horse launched himself at Nikki as if it were she who'd been drowning. Nikki and Horse subsided onto the deck, one sodden tangle of woman and dog. Together.

Tom and Angie hauled themselves up onto the *Lady Nell* as well. Tom tied the lifeboat behind. They'd try and tow it back to harbour but even if they had to let it go it was safer than risking the run back to the *Mary Lou*; another boarding.

The chopper was still overhead. The rest of the boats surrounded them.

The chopper's floodlights lit the scene—woman and dog reunited.

A happy ending.

No, Gabe thought, looking out at the sea of people surrounding him. The sea of people who cared. It was a happy beginning.

These were his people. He belonged.

He and Nikki and Horse…they'd come home.

'Tom,' he called, because he was the head of this fleet and a man had to take a stand some time.

'Yeah?' Tom was watching Nikki hugging Horse, grinning and grinning.

'Come and take this wheel,' Gabe growled. 'There's a woman and a dog I need to hug.'

'I didn't think you did hugging,' Tom said, grinning even more, and Gabe managed a grin back.

'I do now.'

CHAPTER ELEVEN

THE problem with depending on others was sharing. Every single person wanted a piece of happiness.

The boats streamed into the harbour and it seemed half the town was there to greet them—the half who hadn't been out on boats.

Women were fussing over Nikki, hugging her, saying, *Oh, it's a sign that the dog's been saved— you're meant to stay here, dear.*

Henrietta and her troop of dog-lovers were fussing over Horse. Drying him, warming him, giving him warmed feed to settle his stomach. Maybe Nikki needed some of that.

Aggie was there, beaming and beaming.

And the men were fussing over Gabe. Okay, not exactly fussing—Banksia Bay's fishermen didn't do that. They gripped his hand, one after the other, grinning, exultant at their shared triumph. 'Pleasure, mate,' they said almost universally as he tried to thank them, and he knew it was.

This *was* a shared triumph. Sharing. It was a concept he needed to embrace.

But… How soon could he get Nikki alone?

'You want us to whisk you back to Whale Cove?' Harry asked. He'd set the chopper down in the unloading dock and come to share the happy ending. He and his crew were delighted. Without the chopper, they'd never have succeeded.

Without any of these people…

'I hear there's a great honeymoon suite in the Sun Spa resort at Whale Cove,' Harry said reflectively. 'We could whisk you there right now. I'm not sure if they take dogs, though.'

Maybe he'd been looking at Nikki a bit too long, Gabe thought. Maybe what he needed was plain for all to see, for Harry gripped his shoulder and grinned. 'Another one bites the dust. I thought you were a confirmed bachelor, like me. Oh, well, can't win them all. Good luck, mate, welcome to the other side.'

He left, still chuckling.

Others were going, too. Reluctantly. It was after two in the morning.

'You want me to take Horse back to my place and take care of him for the night?' Henrietta asked, and Nikki, a whole six inches from Horse, tugged him closer.

'No. Thank you but…no.'

'Just thought,' Hen said airily. 'Just saying. If you guys need space…'

'We don't need space,' Gabe said and Nikki glanced up at him and he thought…uh-oh.

A man needed to tread warily. He was, after all, the guy who'd refused to fix her pipes—the guy who'd lost her dog.

'I'm hoping we don't need space,' he said.

'You still want to stay the night at my place?' Aggie asked Nikki, and Nikki looked at him—really looked at him. And something changed in her eyes. Something…

'Thank you,' she said. 'But no. Thank you all. You've been absolutely wonderful, but Horse and I need to go home.'

He took her home.

Her side of the house was still sodden. Water was running down her walls. It had been running since they'd left.

There'd be one nightmare of a mess to clear up later, but now…they turned off the water to Nikki's side of the house and let it be.

Who needed two sides to a house anyway?

Nikki was shivering. She hadn't stopped shivering. He whisked her into the bathroom. His bathroom. Ran the bath, good and hot, propelled her in.

'H…Horse…' she muttered.

'I'll take care of Horse,' he said, and it nearly

killed him to leave her but he needed to warm the house.

He stoked up the fire. Made it blaze. Dried Horse with warm towels and more warm towels.

Horse looked devotedly up at him from the fireside. Like: *I'm sorry I caused you trouble but I needed Nikki.*

He and Horse both.

They sat by the fire. Waited.

Nikki came out, wrapped in a towel.

He stood and she walked straight into his arms. He held her close and he knew... This was his woman, his heart, his life.

'I need you,' she whispered and it was an echo of his own heart.

'I've gone about this all the wrong way,' he said into her hair.

'What do you mean?' Their breathing was synchronised. Their heartbeats were synchronised.

'I should have welcomed you with pleasure, cut down the dividing fence, shared Horse, helped with the barbecue, loaned you my mother's books, been proud of you.'

'Nah,' she said. 'I probably would have thought you were wet.' She hesitated. 'Come to think of it, you are wet. I'm warm and dry. You need dry clothes.' But she was still against his heart.

'Not yet. I'm still apologising.'

'There's time to make amends,' she said. 'You can

hug me with pleasure, cut down the dividing fence, share Horse, help with any future barbecues—and I think we should have one soon to thank everyone for tonight—lend me your mother's books, be proud of me. Do you think my apartment's underwater?'

'What's a little water? Nikki, I love you.'

She stilled.

She didn't speak. She just…melted.

He was holding her tight, feeling the warmth of her. Accepting the reality that he was holding the woman of his dreams, right here in his arms.

'I don't suppose you'd consider marriage,' he said and he hadn't known he intended to say it; it was just there.

It shocked them both. She almost dropped the towel. She grabbed it just in time. Made a recovery. Sort of. Took a step back.

'Marriage,' she whispered.

'Just a thought.' He tried to figure how to say all the things that were in his heart and couldn't. Made a bad joke instead. 'It'd make Horse legitimate. You'd be Mum and I'd be Dad.'

She choked. 'You'd marry me—for a dog?'

'I'd marry you for you.'

'You're grumpy.' She was eyeing him with caution now, as if he had the poker.

'Only when hit on the head. I'll try not to be grumpy for anything less.'

'I still want to learn stone walling.'

'I love that you still want to learn stone walling.'

'You go to sea thirteen nights out of fourteen.' She took a deep breath. 'I've learned tonight...I do get seasick.'

'I won't go to sea in rough weather.'

'Promise?'

'Not very rough.'

'Thirteen nights out of fourteen?'

'I'm the fleet owner. I can decide. How about only when I must? And if you were home in my bed... there'd hardly be a must.'

'Of course there would. First hint of a barracuda and out you'd go.'

'Not if you were in my bed.'

'You have a bed on the boat.'

'So I do. But...'

'Then I guess I could take pills and come with you,' she ventured. 'If you'll dig my trenches.'

'Is this business we're talking?'

'I like things to be clear.'

'You want me to find pen and paper and we'll sign stuff before I kiss you?'

'You want to kiss me?'

'More than anything on earth.'

She sighed, a long, drawn-out sigh where things seemed to be let go.

'If I kissed you back I might drop my towel,' she said, smiling and smiling.

'You want to risk it?'

'Horse would be shocked.'

'I believe,' he said softly, in a low, husky growl because that seemed all he was capable of right now, 'I believe our Horse is asleep. Dead to the world.'

'Don't say dead.'

'Alive,' he said, smiling down at her. Smiling and smiling. 'Like I am. I feel more alive right here, right now, than I've ever been in my life. You want to risk the odd towel?'

'I'd risk more than that,' she said, stepping forward, stepping into his arms. 'I'd risk my heart. Or wait…maybe I can't. Maybe my heart's no longer mine to risk.'

It took a while to plan a wedding, mostly because the tiny church on the headland on the far side of Banksia Bay was surrounded by a crumbling stone wall. No one was marrying in that church, Aggie decreed, until the wall was mended, so instead of planning wedding dress, bridesmaids, flowers, Nikki sat on the headland overlooking the sea and fitted stones into a wall that would last for another hundred years.

She loved it—and there was no problem that her attention was focused on the wall, for she had others to do the 'tizzy bits' for her wedding. Aggie and Henrietta and Angie and Hattie and Hilda and Maudie… So many friends.

Her day would be splendid, they decreed, and so it was.

In the end the church was too small. In the end the day was perfect so Gabe stood under frangipani, with the sea as his backdrop, while all the town clustered close by to wait for his bride.

Nikki's parents were here, astounded, bemused, and in the end even confusedly proud that their daughter knew so definitely where she was going, what she was doing.

'She can charge a lot more than she's doing,' her father decreed of his daughter. 'With a skill like this...'

'I can't believe he didn't go to university,' her mother said of Gabe, but they were here, they were smiling, and they'd accepted her new life.

They had no choice, for this *was* Nikki's life. This place. Banksia Bay. Gabe.

A bagpipe sounded, a blast of triumph, and Aggie squeaked in triumph herself. This was her wedding gift, her son the bagpiper, whether Nikki willed it or not.

Nikki did will it. She'd grinned when Aggie had told them. 'Bagpipes,' Gabe had said faintly.

She'd tucked her arm into his and said, 'I won't have it any other way.'

Nikki. His bride.

The bagpipes meant she was here.

Horse was lying beside him, groomed, gleaming, almost handsome. The big dog understood it now, that Gabe and Nikki were one—equals. He'd stay with Gabe or he'd stay with Nikki, but he was only truly content when they were together.

Which was great because that was exactly where Gabe and Nikki intended to be.

Bagpipes. Nikki.

Horse lumbered to his feet and Gabe held his collar. Someone had put a garland of frangipani round Horse's neck. How corny was that?

He loved it.

Then Raff was elbowing him aside, taking Horse's collar firmly in his.

'Priorities, mate,' he said. 'Bride first, dog second.'

He didn't need to be told, for Nikki was here, and he only had eyes for Nikki.

His bride.

Her gown was gorgeous, white silk with an exquisitely beaded bodice and a deceptively simple skirt that draped and flared as if she were floating. She looked as if she was tied to her father's arm to stop her rising. Her hair was beautiful. She'd never again tried to straighten it. Angie had tucked frangipani into her curls.

But Gabe wasn't looking at her hair. He wasn't looking at her gown. He looked only at Nikki. Her smile. Her lovely, lovely smile as she met his gaze, at the shared laughter that was always there. Laughter and love.

He was truly loved.

There was momentary drama. Horse tugged away from Raff and Raff was dumb enough to let him go. But Horse didn't go far. He trod sedately down the carpet they'd laid for the bridal approach, and he greeted his mistress with quiet dignity. Then he turned and walked calmly back to Gabe, preceding the bride.

He glanced around at the congregation as if to say, *See, I know what a real dog should do.* Then he sat beside Gabe to watch.

And watch he did, as his Nikki married her Gabe.

As his mistress found her home.

As life truly began for them all.

* * * * *